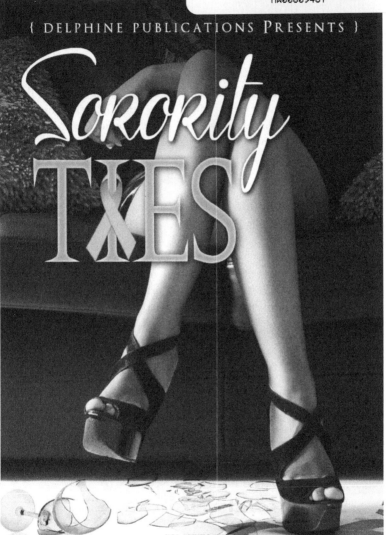

{ DELPHINE PUBLICATIONS Presents }

Sorority TIES

BY AUTHORS

ANNA BLACK, LAKISHA JOHNSON,
TAMMARA MATTHEWS, SAUNDRA,
JAMIE DOSSIE & MELISSA LOVE

Delphine Publications focuses on bringing a reality check to the genre Published by Delphine Publications

Delphine Publications focuses on bringing a reality check to the genre urban literature. All stories are a work of fiction from the authors and are not meant to depict, portray, or represent any particular person Names, characters, places, and incidents are either the product of the author's imagination or are used fictitiously, and any resemblances to an actual person living or dead are entirely coincidental

ISBN: 978-0-9960844-8-2

Edited by: Tee Marshall
Layout: Write On Promotions
Cover Design: Odd Ball Designs

Printed in the United States of America

Sorority Ties

by

The ladies of
Delphine Publications

Chapter 1
Meet Heaven

It's Monday morning and as usual, the animal clinic is filled with animals waiting to be seen. I take a quick glance around the room then immediately head to my office to throw on my lab coat.

"What's on the books for today?" I ask my vet tech, Jewels while looking through a stack of files on my desk. She walks in with a cup of iced coffee and a bagel, then hands it to me.

"I thought that you might need this." She smiles.

"You know me well." I take a sip of the coffee savoring its mocha flavor and sweetness.

"Our first patient of the day is Sparks, a Labrador Retriever who needs to be examined and treated for possible heart worms. Then we have Muffy, a longhaired kitten who needs shots." Jewels handed me a chart with the list of patients for the day.

"Okay then, let's get to work." After seeing a total of five patients, it was now 1:30, so I decided to take a break and soothe the rumbling in my stomach.

"Are you going out for lunch today?" Jewels asked as she popped her head in the door.

"Nope, I got my lunch right here." I pulled a white plastic bag out of my mini-fridge and held it in the air.

"That's too bad, it's nice outside today and the fresh air would do you some good. You want me to bring you something back?"

"No I'm fine, thanks anyway." As I sat down, I spread the contents of my lunch across my desk then frowned at the peanut butter and jelly sandwich that I threw together this morning in a rush. Maybe I should go out and get something to eat. I packed my lunch back up, threw it back into the mini-fridge and took off my lab coat. I really could use some fresh air, a mocha Frappuccino wouldn't hurt either. As I made my way out of the door and down the street, I ran into Jewels.

"I see you decided to come out after all, huh?"

"Yeah that peanut butter and jelly sandwich wasn't looking to hot." We laughed. "Where you headed?"

"To that new coffee shop down the street."

"Didn't you already have coffee this morning?" Jewels joked.

"Yes but now I need a Frappuccino."

"Fine. I guess I'll walk with you."

As I stood in the line waiting to order, Jewels tapped me on the shoulder.

"Do you know that guy over there?"

Confused, I looked over. "Who?"

"The guy in the grey suit and blue shirt. He keeps staring at you."

"As far as I know, I don't." I turned back around and moved forward since I was next in line.

"He's still starring at you. That's just weird, why doesn't he just say something."

I looked over in his direction again, but this time he turned his head away as if he were shy.

"See he's playing games cuz he damn sure ain't shy the way he's been eyeballing you."

I laughed at the screwed up face that Jewels made.

"Good afternoon ma'am, what would you like to order."

"Um can I get a mocha Frappuccino with whipped cream."

"Yes ma'am, anything else?"

"Let me get a cinnamon walnut strudel as well." I paid for my food and moved over to the side to wait.

"There he goes again looking." Jewels said to me, shaking her head. This time I looked over and studied him for a minute. Indeed, he was a handsome man. Standing about 6'1 with brown eyes, a medium muscular build, skin the color of milk chocolate and a low fade, this man was the epitome of fine, or at least in my eyes he was. He glimpsed over in my direction and we locked eyes. Tired of playing the cat and mouse game. I gave him a soft smile and slight wave. He waved back and smiled as well, displaying a nice set of teeth.

"Mocha Frappuccino!" A lady yelled from behind the counter. I briskly walked up to grab my drink and so did he.

"Oh I'm sorry, I thought this one was mine." I looked at him confused.

"It's okay, it's a popular drink."

"I know. I just didn't expect you to be getting the same thing, I guess I thought you'd be ordering something stronger or different."

"Meaning?" He looked at me with his eyebrows raised.

3

"It's just that you're so manly for such a feminine drink." Jewels busted out laughing. I looked at her and she looked back sheepishly. Turning my attention back to Mr. Handsome, he starred at me.

"So what? You think I'm gay because I ordered a certain drink? I didn't know coffee drinks came with sex labels."

"I'm sorry. I didn't mean it like that, it's just that you don't see many men drinking these."

"I think your drink's ready." Jewels interjected in an attempt to save me from further embarrassment. I grabbed my drink and headed towards the door with my tail tucked between my legs and Jewels on my heels. Squeezing through the long line of customers, I felt someone grab my hand as I released the door. As I turned around, I came face to face with none other than Mr. Handsome. I sighed.

"So do you always run off so quickly after insulting people?"

"No and I apologize, I didn't mean to insult you."

"It's fine, but for the record, it's not good to make assumptions."

"I guess not." I looked down at the ground to avoid eye contact.

"How about this, let's start over. I'm Quinton and you are?" He extended his hand to me. "Heaven, my name is Heaven." I extended my hand for him to shake.

"That's a nice name," he smiled, "so can I take you out some time?"

"I'm not sure about that, I'm really busy with work."

"Ok, well how about we meet for lunch?"

4

This man sure is persistent. "I barely get a lunch."

"So now you blow me off after the insults?"

"No, you're a good looking man…"

"Then what's the problem?" He looked at me confused.

"You'll have time tomorrow." Jewels chimed in with a big smile on her face. I cut my eyes at her.

"No, I don't."

"Yes, you do. You don't have an appointment on the books until 1pm." What the hell? She's supposed to be on my side. We're definitely having a talk about this when we get back to the office.

"So, since you're free in the morning, how about we meet up for coffee?"

Backed into a corner, thanks to Jewels' big mouth, I practically had no choice but to agree.

"Sure that'll be fine." I plastered on a fake smile.

"Here's my card. We can meet here around ten, will that work for you?"

"Yeah that's fine."

"Alright then, take care Miss Lady. I'll see you in the morning."

I watched Quinton walk away then looked at Jewels through squinted eyes.

"So what the hell was that? Did y'all concoct this plan against me before I got there or something?"

"Me speaka no engles."

"Jewels don't play with me." I chased behind her as she briskly walked ahead of me. Once we were in the office we ate our lunch then it was back to work. After completing the last few appointments of the day, I started in on her again.

"So are you gonna answer me?"

"I didn't plan on it, but since you asked, I did it because you need to get out and date."

"I told you, I'm not interested in dating anyone. Why can't y'all understand that."

"Ok, who is y'all?"

"You, my family, and my sorority sisters!"

"Because we want you to be happy."

"I am happy. I love my career and my life, especially without having to worry about a damn man."

"Heaven, you can't let your past relationship with Lamar dictate your future. Every man isn't like him."

"I understand that but I'm not looking to find out either."

"You are such a prude, I swear. Eventually you're gonna have to get back out on the dating scene. You can't hide behind your job forever."

"I'm fine with the way things are, but now thanks to you I'm stuck meeting up with this dude that I really don't want to meet with."

"Girl please... if you don't meet with him, I will cuz I promise you, no other woman would pass him up."

"That's them, I'm not every other woman. I'm not desperate to have a man"

"Girl, you betta get your mind right. Those looks ain't gon last forever, so you better get 'em while you still can."

I sighed and plopped down in the seat behind my desk. I was lost in thought when I looked up and saw Jewels standing there staring at me with her hands on her hips. It was if she was reading my mind. "You better not stand that man up. If you do I will meet him myself and give him your number."

"What are you talking about?" I looked at her with confusion on my face.

"You know exactly what I'm talking about. Don't show up and you'll see."

With that, Jewels headed towards the door. "I'll see you in the morning and be safe." Half way out the door, she stopped and turned back towards me. "And wear something cute."

"What's wrong with what I have on now?" I looked down at my outfit.

"You look like somebody's grandma. Try to go for the sexy librarian look, guys like that. Good night."

Chapter 2

The Meeting

The next morning, I woke up irritated and not wanting to be bothered. Fine day to meet up for a coffee date, I grimaced. Slowly, I sifted through my closet and decided on what to wear. I guess this will do. I pulled out a pencil skirt with a slight split up the back and a pinstriped blouse that dipped slightly in the front to display just enough cleavage. I'll top it off with a pair of black peep toe pumps. After showering and doing my hair and makeup I headed out the door wishing that I could cancel our plans. Once I made it in front of the coffee house and parked, I eased out of my car and adjusted my outfit.

"Hey Ms. Lady, I'm glad you could make it. I thought you were gonna stand me up for a minute." He displayed that beautiful smile of his and immediately I began to feel a nervous sensation in the pit of my stomach.

"No, I wouldn't do that to you, especially after the way I insulted you yesterday. The least I could do is show up."

We walked toward the door and he stopped and opened it for me. I smiled.

"A gentleman, you don't see many of those nowadays."

"That's because we're a dying breed. I'm one of the few left."

After ordering our breakfast, we found a table in a quiet corner of the room.

"So what do you do?" He asked me.

"Wow! You get right down to business, don't you?" We laughed. "I'm a veterinarian. I work at the animal clinic up the street from here."

"That's an interesting job. You're the first vet that I've dated."

"Who said we're dating? I thought we were just having coffee." I looked at him.

"I mean you're the first woman that I've met with that job title."

"I know what you meant, I'm just messing with you." I smiled at his boyish charm. We sat and got to know each other a little better. Admittedly, I was having a great time until the dreaded question was asked.

"So have you ever been married or are you involved with anyone?"

"No not currently."

"Can I see you again?"

"I don't know, I'm not really interested in dating anyone right now. I just got out of a serious relationship."

"We don't have to get into anything serious. I just want to go out again."

I sighed as I toyed with my silverware. "Are you seeing anyone right now?"

He stalled.

"Is that a yes?"

"I'm kinda dating someone, but it's not serious."

"What is considered not serious?" I stared at him as he processed his next response.

"The lady that I'm dating doesn't even know my real name. Mostly everything that I've told her thus far has been a lie."

"Ok, so how do I know you're not lying to me?" He opened up his wallet, pulled out his driver's license and handed it to me. I reviewed the information on it and handed it back to him.

"So what makes me so special? As far as I know, you could tell this to every woman you meet."

"I like how reserved you are. The woman that I'm currently seeing isn't like that."

"So what is she like?"

"A hoodrat. Now don't get me wrong, she got brains, but conservative she is not. I like my women like you. I know I haven't known you long, but I like your demeanor." He starred at me and I could feel my palms begin to sweat. I looked down at my watch.

"I think I have to get going. I have a patient soon."

"It's only 11 o'clock."

"I know but I have to have time to prep. It takes a minute to do that." He knew I was bullshitting, but thankfully he didn't call me on it.

"Okay, let me get your number. Maybe I can hit you up this evening after you get off work or something."

"My phone hasn't been working right lately. Actually, I'm supposed to be taking it back to the store today to try to get a new one. I barely even get calls." Just as luck would have it, my phone rang at that very moment. Dammit!

"I thought your phone didn't work."

"I guess this is one of the few occasions where it is." I laughed nervously.

Feeling like an idiot, I went ahead and wrote down my number then gave it to him.

"Are you sure you want to give me this, you sure went through a lot of trouble making up that lie to keep me from getting it."

"I ... just—I"

"Don't worry about it. Clearly you're uncomfortable with the whole dating thing, so just call me when you're ready." He handed me my number back then got up from the table.

"We should probably head out, you don't want to keep your patient waiting."

"Um yeah, right." I got up from the table and he walked with me outside.

"It was nice meeting you, Heaven. Maybe one day we'll meet again under better circumstances."

"Maybe so." We parted ways and I headed back to my office embarrassed and feeling like shit. How could I have been so ignorant towards him? Maybe I'll call him later to apologize.

Later on that day after a long day of work, I sat at home starring at the card that Quinton gave me with his number on it. Debating on whether I should call him or not, I picked up the phone, but quickly hung it back up. Just call the man what's the worst that could happen. I thought to myself. Finally building up the courage, I picked up the phone again and dialed his number. After three rings, I heard his deep husky voice on the other end.

"Um hi, this is Heaven did I call at a bad time?"

"Naw, you good, I was just working out. What's up?"

"Well, I wanted to call and apologize for earlier. I didn't mean to come off like such a bitch. I just haven't been out with anyone in a while so I got a little freaked out."

"You good, I just figured you didn't wanna be bothered."

"No, honestly I really enjoyed your company and I'd love to hang out again."

I heard silence on the other end and hoped I hadn't messed things up to the point where he didn't want to see me again.

"Quinton?"

"Yeah I'm still here, I was just grabbing some water. So you said you want to meet up again?"

"Yes."

"That's cool, how about Friday night, we can go see a movie and grab a bite to eat."

"Friday is fine."

"Ok cool, I'll pick you up around six-thirty."

"Great. I'll let you get back to your workout."

"Why the rush, we can talk longer if you want to."

I smiled as that nervous feeling returned to the pit of my stomach.

"Ok, I don't mind talking for a bit. I got all night."

Chapter 3

Girls Night Out

It's Thursday night and as usual I meet up with my sorority sisters, April, Delilah, Stephanie, Eve and Keli for a girl's night out. Clubbing isn't our thing so we invented the girls' night out as a way to hang out and have fun. We agreed to rotate houses every other Thursday night to make things fair, and then we'd play games, talk, sip on wine, and watch movies. This specific evening, we sat around my living room in a circle sipping on wine and conversing about the men that we're currently dating or married to.

"Girl, I'm telling you he put it on me last night!" Keli said clapping and throwing her hands in the air as we all laughed at her dramatics.

"He had my toes curling and me pleading for mercy!"

"Now that's what I'm talking about!" April chimed in and gave Keli a high five. "Don't be wasting my time! If you gon do it, do it right." We all laughed.

"So Heaven, I heard you got a new man, do give us details." Keli took a sip of her wine then gave me a sly smile.

I adjusted myself in my seat and smiled coyly.

"Well ladies, if you must know, yes I do have a new man, possibly. His name is Quinton and so far he's wonderful. I met him a week ago at the coffeehouse down the street from my job."

"Oh really? Why didn't we hear about Mr. Right last week?" April asked with her lips poked out.

"Because I wasn't sure about him at first. Now may I finish?" I rolled my eyes playfully and laughed lightly.

"Now as I was saying, while I was standing off to the side waiting for my mocha Frappuccino, we ended up trying to grab the same drink and from there the conversation began. On my way out the door he stopped me and asked me out then gave me his number and the rest is history."

"Have y'all been out on a date yet?" Delilah asked me.

"Yes, he took me to a movie and this really nice Italian restaurant that he said had just opened up."

"How was the food?" Eve asked.

"The hell with that, how was the date?" Stephanie asked waving off Eve's question.

"The food and the date were great. We talked about everything from our childhoods to politics. I really enjoyed his company."

"So how does he look?" Keli quizzed.

"He's about 6'1 with dark brown eyes, caramel skin, muscular build, and a nice smile."

"Ooh he sounds fine. You got a picture of him?"

"Actually I think I do, he texted me one last night."

They all gathered around me as I searched through my phone for his picture. "Here he is." I smiled then held the phone out so they could see him.

"Humph, he sure is fine." Keli replied

I noticed the lustful look on her face and immediately felt my temper begin to flare.

"He looks real familiar, what did you say his name is?" Keli asked me.

"Quinton."

"That's interesting he looks just like this dude I've been dealing with."

I snatched the phone out her hand and frowned.

"Well I'm sure this isn't him." I looked at her annoyed

"Fo real though, he looks just like this dude I met leaving your job one day after having lunch with you."

The more Keli talked, the more I wanted to punch her in the mouth. I don't know why I felt so defensive over this dude, but I was pissed. Ain't nothing worse than one of your friends looking at your man like a Thanksgiving dinner right in front of your face. I'll definitely be watching this bitch around him.

The rest of the night went by pretty quick and honestly I couldn't wait for it to be over so I could call Quinton. I needed to find out if this was the woman that he said he was dating because if so we wouldn't work out. I've never been into dating my friends' men or leftovers. I'm just not that type. Besides, we vowed that we'd never let a man come between us and I planned to keep that promise.

Happy that the night was over, I called Quinton.

"So how was your girls' night out?"

"It was cool, I gotta ask you something though."

"Ok what's up?"

"Who is the girl you're dating, what is her name?"

"Why you wanna know that?"

"I'm just curious."

Quinton got silent for a minute.

"Well?"

"Her name is Keli. I met her near the coffee shop."

"Thank you for being honest."

"Why do you say that?"

"Because I know her, we're friends."

"Okay, so what's that got to do with you?"

"I can't date you. It wouldn't be right."

"I told you that I'm not serious about her."

"I understand that, but she's still my friend."

"So you're not going to go out with me anymore?"

"No, I'm sorry."

"Do you want me to stop seeing her?"

"No, you were seeing her first."

Quinton and I went back and forth for a while about my decision and still he refused to let it go. Tired of talking about it, I decided to get off the phone in hopes that he'd just move on. As I lay in my bed I starred at the ceiling and wondered if I was making the right decision. My heart was telling me go with it, but my head was telling me to move on. Listening to my head, I decided to move on. There are plenty of other fish in the sea so there's no point of fighting over one man.

Chapter 4

Promise Broken

The next morning, I woke up a bit saddened by my decision but at the same time I felt relieved and happy that I was able to stick to my guns. Deciding once again that my material possessions and job were all I needed, I put a smile on my face and headed into work.

"You seem happy today, your new man must've worked you out last night!" Jewels said as she walked in my office.

"Actually no, there is no new man."

"What you mean?"

"I found out that he's been seeing Keli."

"How did that happen?"

"He met her near the coffee shop one day after she left here and I guess they've been messing around ever since."

"Is she serious about him?"

"I doubt it, but if she had him I don't want him."

"Damn it's a small world." Jewels shook her head as she headed back out front.

A few minutes later she returned with a dozen roses in her hand.

"Oh those are nice who sent them to you?"

"They're not for me, they're for you." Jewels said handing them to me. Immediately, I knew they were from Quinton.

"You must've made a big impression on ole boy. He's sending you roses and everything."

"I told him to move on."

"Well, apparently he didn't get the message."

"I guess not." I put the flowers in water and sat them on my desk.

"So what are you gonna do? Are you gonna call and thank him?"

"Hell no, then he's gonna think we're good."

"Girl, you crazy! I'd be like, to hell with Keli and see him anyway. You a damn good friend, cuz it sure couldn't be me."

"Well I'm not the type to share. Plus we've been friends for too long to ruin it over some man."

"I guess." Jewels smirked.

"I'm a go ahead and set up for the next patient."

Around lunchtime, Jewels went out to grab something as usual, but I decided to stay in. I was fearful that I might run into Quinton. Like last time, I unpacked my peanut butter and jelly sandwich to eat. Before I could take a bite, one of the other doctors told me that I had a visitor up front." Dammit, I can never eat in peace. I wrapped my sandwich back up, tossed it in the bag, then headed up front. I looked around the room and saw Quinton standing by the front entrance with a bag of food in his hand.

"What are you doing here?"

"Bringing you lunch. I thought you might be hungry."

"That's sweet of you, but I told you that I can't see you anymore."

"I know that's what your mouth said, but I can tell that's not what your heart wants."

18

"And how would you know?"

"I can see it in your eyes." I blushed as he held my chin in his hands. This guy was taking a toll on me. I wanted to turn him away so bad, but he was making it so hard.

"You have to leave." I turned to walk away but he grabbed my hand.

"It's only lunch. There's no point of letting it go to waste."

He had a point. It was either this or the peanut butter and jelly sandwich. I choose this.

"Okay, lunch and that's it."

"That's all I'm asking for." He smiled once again causing those butterflies to dance around in my stomach. Damn, this man is killing me.

After that one day it became a ritual of him sending me flowers and bringing me lunch. His intention was to wear me down, but today I planned on putting a stop to it. It's been three weeks too long. Today Quinton walked in looking handsome as ever.

"Hey, I brought us some Chinese food."

"Oh that's cool. Thanks." He followed me back to my office.

As we sat down to eat, he starred at me.

"What's wrong? You don't like Chinese?"

"Not particularly, but that's not the problem."

"Okay then what's up?"

"I really have to end this." I blurted out.

"You don't wanna do that."

"Yes I do Quinton, it's not right."

Quinton stood up, walked over to me and pulled me up out of my chair.

"You want me just as much as I want you, you just don't want to admit it."

"You are so full of yourself Quinton, you can't tell me what I…"

Before I could say another word, he kissed me causing my knees to go weak.

Damn that felt so good. I couldn't even remember what I was about to say.

"You good?" He smiled down at me.

"Yeah I'm good, just taking it all in."

"So you still want me to leave?"

"No."

We finished eating then Quinton left, leaving me to justify my feelings for him.

"Hey! How was lunch with Mr. Handsome." Jewels asked with a smile plastered on her face.

"It was great."

"So are you gonna see him again?"

"I think so."

"That's what I'm talking bout! Fuck Keli."

"She's still my friend, Jewels."

"So, the way you said she was acting when she saw his picture should make you rethink that. Hell, she ratchet anyway. I'm sure she ain't gonna miss him as many dudes as she mess with."

"Yeah that's true. It don't seem like he's serious about her no way. He didn't even give her his real name."

"Ain't she the one who tried to holla at Lamar when y'all was dating?"

"Yep."

"And you still calling this broad your friend? You crazy as hell."

"I'm over that. Lamar wasn't shit anyway."

"All I can say is watch her, cause I guarantee you the moment she finds out y'all dating she's gonna be trying all kinds of shit to get at him. And don't trust him either, watch him too."

The next day the girls and I met up at the mall.

"Hey what's up?" We all hugged and said our hellos.

We talked for a minute about random stuff, then the real questions came.

"So how are things going with you and that dude you dating?" Keli asked me

"Things are great, why you ask?"

"Just curious."

"Why are you always the first one to ask me about him?"

"Because I think it's nice that you finally found someone to make you happy."

"Sure you are, the same way you were happy for me when me and Lamar were together."

"What's that supposed to mean?"

"Absolutely nothing," I smirked

"Why are you even bringing up Lamar? He has nothing to do with this."

"Because I know you. You were the same way when me and him first started dating."

"What's your damn problem?"

21

"Come on y'all stop trippin, we're supposed to be hanging out and having a good time." Eve said, stepping in between us.

We walked in silence for a minute.

"So whose house is the Girls Night Out at this week?" April asked, breaking the silence.

"Yours." We said in unison.

"And don't be trying to be cheap on the food and liquor this time either cuz lord knows your ass will serve us some cheese wiz and crackers in a heart beat." We all laughed.

"Hey, times are hard I ain't got time to be spending everything I got on one night of fun." April replied.

"I feel her cuz I know I went straight to the discount store to get all those snacks y'all were chowing down on at my house."

We spent the rest of the evening laughing and enjoying our time together.

Chapter 5

Meet April

"Ladies, this has been fun but I'm going to head out." I said.

"Dang, why you rushing? You ain't got nobody at home waiting on you?" Stephanie said. "Sit your ass down."

"How do you know? I could have your husband waiting on me!" I returned.

"Girl, please! I am not worried because Drew wouldn't do anything like that. Hell, look at all this and then look at you!" She said moving her hand down her body. "No offense, but why would he cheat when I look this good?"

"Because then open that mouth of yours!" I said, getting pissed.

"Damn!" Keli laughed.

"I'll see y'all Thursday." I said. Who in the hell does she think she is? I mumbled as I walked to the car. Look at all this! Like she's the finest woman walking. Whatever!

I rushed home because, little did they know, I did have a date. I laid out the new panty and bra set that he bought me as a gift as I ran for the shower. As soon as I finished getting dressed and oiling my body, I heard the doorbell.

"Coming" I yelled.

I opened the door and he looked good enough to eat.

"Dang girl, did you get dressed up for me?"

"Of course I did, come in." I said, stepping back to let him in as he handed me a dozen of roses.

"These are beautiful but you didn't have to do this, I've told you that a hundred times."

"I know, but I like pampering you because you make it so easy."

"Well, then I'll stop complaining. You want anything to drink?"

"All I want is you."

"Well, let me put these in some water and I'll meet you in the bedroom, you know where it is."

"Ok, but I'm going to take a quick shower."

I went into the kitchen and replaced the roses he bought me last week with the ones from tonight. I walked back to the bedroom and heard the water running in the shower. I went over to my iPod and set my playlist to shuffle. Rocket by Beyoncé started playing as I lit the candles that were already placed around the room and I set the massage oil on the night stand. I pulled the covers back on the bed and turned out the lights just as he walked out of the bathroom with a towel wrapped around his waist.

"Come here and lie down." I ordered.

"Babe, if you keep spoiling me, you're going to make it hard for me to go home."

"I'm only treating you as good as you treat me." I smiled. "Now, turn on your back."

I grabbed the oil and climbed on top of him pouring some in my hands. I started massaging him from the neck down. I moved down to his waist and removed the towel. He moaned which made me smile. I continued moving down until he grabbed my hand. He pulled me up to him as I took his mouth into mine. I felt his hardness against me, so I grind into him. He moved his hand down and snatched the panties that I had on off, destroying them. "I'll replace them," He said as he started to enter me.

"Hold up!" I said, reaching over to pull out the drawer. I grabbed a condom and slid down to put it on him. I took him into my mouth and then released him and slid the condom on. I moved and slowly slid down on him as I leaned back to take him all in. I began to work my magic as he grabbed my waist causing me to tighten up and move faster. He turned me over and pushed my legs over his shoulders as he thrust into me. "OOO, don't stop," I moaned. His pace quickened as I squeezed him tighter. I wrapped my legs around him as we rocked into our climax together. He fell over next to me pulling me into him. "Damn Drew, I needed that!" I said snuggling closer to him. "You better not fall asleep because you know Stephanie will be calling soon."

"Please don't remind me April."

Chapter 6

The next day

I made it to work early the next morning with a smile on my face. I was humming as I made it to my office. As soon as I threw my bags down on the desk my phone rung, "Brown and Garner Law Office, this is April."

"Hey girl, you're there early."

"Hey Stephanie, what's up." I ask a little dry.

"I wanted to call and apologize for last night. I shouldn't have said what I did and I'm sorry."

"Oh, it's cool. I didn't take offense to that." I said smiling.

"I just wanted to make sure. I can get beside myself sometime, so I just wanted to clear the air. Do you need me to bring anything over on Thursday?"

"No, I have everything covered."

"Ok girl, I'll see you Thursday."

"Yea, see you then." I hung up without even saying goodbye. Hell, she gets on my nerves, always thinking she knows everything. Plus I have too much work to do than to worry about Stephanie's stuck up ass.

I finished up some paperwork for some of the partners, and it was already lunch time. I grabbed my purse to head out for an hour just as my cellphone rang. I rolled my eyes as the caller id showed my mother's phone number.

"Hello."

"Don't be answering the phone like you don't want to be bothered, why didn't you come over yesterday?"

"Hey to you too momma, I was busy."

"Too busy to brang your ass over here to check on me?"

"Momma, I'm at work, is anything wrong?"

"Naw, but I need some cigarettes and a few groceries."

"I just gave you money 3 days ago for groceries and I am not buying you cigarettes. That's why you're in the shape you're in now."

"Don't worry about what shape I'm in. I've been smoking for as long as I can remember and it ain't killed me yet and I gave that money to your brother to get his car fixed."

"Are you freaking kidding me? Momma, he stays there with you for free and you give him the grocery money to fix his car?"

"He needs his car because he has to go to court tomorrow. You know that girl is trying to put him on child support."

"Look momma, I'll be over there later to bring you some groceries, but I will not give you any more money to give to James. He's a grown man, let him fend for himself. I have to go, I'll see you later." I hung up before she could answer. I hate to talk to her like that but she drives me crazy.

I was still mumbling to myself when I bumped into Gerald coming out of my office.

"Dang Ms. Paralegal, what's up with you?"

"I'm sorry Gerald, I wasn't paying attention."

"It's cool. You headed out?"

"Yea, did you need anything?"

"No, I was coming to see if you wanted to go to lunch."

"Lunch?"

"Yea, you're saying it like it's something disgusting." He laughed.

"No, no, you just caught me off guard but sure, lunch will be great. Let me grab my jacket and I'll meet you at the elevators."

I was smiling hard as I hurried back to get my jacket. I walked out to see some of the others girls in the office rolling their eyes at me and that made me switch a little harder. I knew that they were hating because Gerald was one of the partners in the firm, he is single and fine!

"You ready?" I asked a little loud for their pleasure.

"I sure am." He replied back putting his hand on the small of my back as the elevator doors opened.

Gerald took me to this sushi restaurant not far from the office. We were having a nice lunch and the conversation was actually good. I got to know him on a personal level and I was actually shocked because I had judged him as a ladies man.

"What are you smiling about?" He asked.

"Oh, I didn't realize I was." I said embarrassed.

"You were and I hope it was for me."

"It was, um, I'm actually surprised by you."

"Is that a good or bad thing?"

"Good, because I thought you were a ladies man but this conversation has me changing my mind."

"Wow, you judged me? I'm hurt."

I laughed just as my phone vibrated. "Excuse me, I need to get this call." I got up to walk to the bathroom.

"Hello"

"You're out on a lunch date?"

"Excuse you?"

"April, don't play with me. Are you on a lunch date?"

"Drew, you have no reason to question me. Is this why you called me? By the way, how did you know I was out having lunch?"

"That doesn't matter. What is going on?"

"What do you mean? I'm having lunch."

"I'm talking about with us. You slept with me last night and then you're out on a date the next day."

"Whoa, hold up! You are not my man. You go home to your wife at night and that doesn't give you the right to question me. Now, if we are going to have a problem, then let's end this now. Call me back when you decide because I have to go."

I hung up the phone and walked back to the table.

"Everything ok?"

"Yes, everything is fine. Where were we?"

We finished lunch and drove back to the office. Of course, those same heifers had their eyes glued to me so I made sure to wear the biggest smile and switch even harder. I walked into my office and closed the door before laughing at their asses. I sat down at my desk and an instant message popped up from Gerald.

"Thank you for a wonderful lunch. I hope we can do dinner soon."

I was actually jumping up and down in my office, thanking God he couldn't see me. "Of course, I'd like that. Let me know when." I included my number and pressed send.

"Great! I will definitely call you later tonight."

29

"I look forward to it."

Chapter 7

Girls Night

Leaving work, I cringed, because Drew kept calling and of course, I was ignoring him. He had the nerve to question me about who I'm having lunch with and he has a wife at home. Man please! I was glad to be off though because it gave me a chance to stop by the store, my mom's house and to get everything together for girls night because the last thing I needed was these heifers talking about the food and drinks.

"Mom! Mom, where are you?"

"Girl, why in the hell are you screaming like you're crazy? With all that noise, you'll wake the dead."

"I called you a few times and you didn't answer. I put your groceries in the kitchen." I said getting ready to go.

"Why are you in such a rush, you got a new man?"

"No, but I'm having girls night at my house and I have to make a few stops before I get home."

"You still hanging out with them heifers?"

"Momma, don't start. Those are my friends."

"If that's what you call them."

"I gotta go. I'll call you tomorrow."

I left before she started in on my friends. She has never cared for them and she made it known every time I mentioned them. Shoot, I still had stuff to do and stopping by here put me way behind. I stopped at the liquor store and got 4 bottles of wine and some Patron because with Keli and Heaven's drama, all of it was definitely going to be needed. I didn't feel like cooking, so I decided to stop by Olive Garden and order some pasta and salad. Yes, I can cook, but I'm tired. I made it home and put the wine on ice, the salad in the refrigerator and the pasta on the stove. I turned on the oven to make some brownies for dessert when I realized that I only had 20 minutes to shower and change. As soon as I made it to the bedroom my phone rang.

"Yes," I answered with an attitude.

"Why have you been ignoring my calls?"

"Because I don't want to talk."

"So, you go on a lunch date and now I don't matter?"

"It's not about who I have lunch with, it's about you trying to control my life."

"It is about who you have lunch with, you shouldn't be having lunch with anyone else. Are you having sex with this dude?"

"First of all, you sound crazy. Secondly, I can have lunch, dinner and sex with whoever I want. I don't belong to you and you damn sure don't belong to me. Question your wife, Drew, not me!" I hung up the phone and turned the water on for my shower.

I finished getting dressed just as the doorbell rang. I just knew it was Delilah because she is always on time but to my surprise, it was Stephanie.

"Hey girl, I thought you were Delilah."

"I beat Delilah? She is going to be pissed." She said laughing.

"I know right. Come on in, I was about to put some brownies in the oven and warm the pasta."

"Pasta? You cooked pasta?"

"Hell no, I ordered it." I laughed.

"I should have known." She said as the doorbell rang again.

"Whatever, go answer the door."

All the girls finally made it and we were actually having a great time, drama free. After eating, we are sitting around laughing, talking and of course, drinking when Keli started.

"So Heaven, how are things with our boyfriend?" She said, downing a shot.

"Keli, please don't start that crap tonight." Heaven replied.

"Start what? I was just asking." Keli laughed.

"No, you were just starting some mess." I said.

"Whatever! She can't be mad at me, I was seeing him first." Keli said.

"First off, he pursued me. Second, you didn't even know his real name so, how could you actually be dating? And third, if it is so serious between you two, then why hasn't he said that?" Heaven asked.

"I didn't say dating boo, I said seeing. As in sex and an occasional dinner. Regardless of it being serious or not, isn't there a girl code that says you shouldn't mess with someone a friend has been with?"

"Girl, you know you are sleeping with him and probably 10 others. If we depend on you, there will never be anyone else to date." Stephanie butted in.

"Who in the fuck asked you anything? Why don't you worry about who your husband is sleeping with?" Keli snapped.

I almost choked on my wine. "Keli! Why would you even say that?"

"Because she should mine her own business. She's always putting her nose in everybody else business, mind your own!" Keli shouted pointing at Stephanie.

"Fuck you, Keli!" Stephanie screamed. "You don't know nothing about my husband. You're just mad because he won't look at your ratchet ass!"

"If he's married to you then he's definitely cheating to stay sane. Hell, you probably tell him when to have sex and the exact time to cum, don't you?" Keli laughed before taking another shot of Patron.

Before anyone else had a chance to say anything, Stephanie jumped up and threw her drink in Keli's face. Eve and Delilah jumped in between them to keep them from coming to blows, but Keli wiped her face and laughed. "Is that all you got Ms. High and Mighty? The truth hurts doesn't it?"

"Keli, stop it! Why are you acting like this?" Eve asked.

"Be for real! All y'all know that Stephanie thinks she's better than everybody else. She walks her stuck up ass around here with her head so high in the air that she doesn't even see that her house is crumbling. Oh, but who is going to believe old ratchet Keli? Yea, I may sleep around, but I am not dumb. Open your eyes sweetie." Keli said getting a paper towel.

"I'm going to go because the last thing I need is some ghetto chick trying to tell me about my life. I know my husband doesn't cheat. Why would he when he has me? And if you think I am going to let you shake me, you can think again. You may not be dumb, but what man would want you after you open your mouth?" Stephanie said looking at Keli. "It's best you stay away from me before I have to put my hands on you."

"Annndd? Am I supposed to be scared? All I have to do is break one of your nails and you're done!" Keli laughed.

"Stop this! Keli, you need to leave. GO!" I said pointing towards the door.

"With pleasure. Heaven, kiss our boo for me tonight, ok?"

"What is wrong with that girl? I mean, I've seen her in true Keli form before, but tonight she was really in it?" Delilah said.

"I don't know but this is crazy. How in the hell can we continue to have girls night with this mess?" I said picking up a glass from the table. "I'm going to clean up."

"You need some help?" Heaven asked.

"No, you ladies go ahead. I'll finish up here. After all this drama, I'm ready to go to bed."

"Me too. I'll talk to you all tomorrow." Stephanie said grabbing her purse.

What in the hell is Keli's problem? I thought as I cleaned the kitchen and living room.

I had just turned off all the lights and positioned myself in bed with my Kindle when my phone vibrated. Lord, please don't let this be Drew, I said out loud but it was a number that I didn't know. I wasn't going to answer it until whoever it was called right back.

"Hello"

"Hey, April, this is Gerald."

"Oh, hey."

"I'm sorry, did I wake you?" He asked because of the sound of my voice I assumed.

"No, it's cool. I was still up. I just didn't know your number. What's up?"

"I was just calling to chat with you, but if it's too late we can talk another time."

"No, you're fine. I was just about to read a book, but now you have my full attention." I smiled. Did I really just say that?

"Your full attention, huh? I like that. I was just sitting here thinking about you so I decided to call."

"And what were you thinking?"

"That I'd really like to see you again."

"You see me almost every day at work."

"Yea, I know, but I'm talking about outside of work. You know like a date with just you and me."

"Oh and when would you like to go out on a date?"

"How about Friday?"

"As in tomorrow?"

He laughed, "Yea, is that too soon?"

"No," I cleared my throat.

"But? What is it April? You can be honest with me."

"It's just that I recently got out of a relationship that really left me hurt and I don't want to be hurt again. I know that you can have any girl at the office, why me?"

"Yes, I can have any girl but I don't want a girl, I want a woman which is why I chose you. Listen, I cannot speak on the thing that hurt you in the past and I can't promise you that I won't make some mistakes because I'm human, but I have no intentions of hurting you. I don't know where this will go, so let's just take it slow, is that cool?"

Damn! "Hell yes!" I said before I could catch myself and we both burst out laughing.

"Good, now tell me about April."

"Well, I'm 29, no kids, I come from a huge dysfunctional family, I was engaged but he cheated and you know where I work so yea that's it. Now, tell me about Gerald."

"I'm 35, no kids, I also come from a huge crazy family, was married once but now I'm divorced. I love life and I also noticed that about you. It's actually one of the things that drew me to you."

"Good to know. What else have you noticed about me?"

"That you are a beautiful woman!" I could tell he was smiling.

"And?"

"Dang, you're going to put a brother on the spot like that? Ok, well I also noticed your small lips that I cannot wait to kiss, your waist that I can't wait to hold and your ass that I cannot wait to spank!"

Whew Lord! I had to throw the covers back because I was starting to sweat!

"Ok, Ok! You got me speechless and that's rare, but I like it."

We talked for over 2 hours and I must say that I liked him because he is not the person I had pegged him to be. I am really interested in seeing where this will go.

Chapter 8

Date Night

I woke up with a smile on my face as I got ready for work. On my way, I made my usual stop by Starbucks for my caramel latte and as soon as I stepped to the side to wait I noticed Jared, Eve's fiancé walk in. I was just about to go over and speak when I see a young lady walk over to him and kiss him on the mouth. What the hell?" I mumble as I grabbed my phone to snap a picture.

"April, caramel latte!"

I walk over to get my coffee and purposely walk his way to speak.

"What's up Jared?"

"April, uh, hey! What you doing out this way?" He stuttered.

"Getting coffee. Tell Eve I said to call me." I said walking out the door. I made sure to throw that in to make his ass squirm. I had no intentions on telling Eve because women can get territorial over their man and they'll be quick to believe him over the friend that they've had for years so, for the moment I'll just hold on to this information until the right time.

I pulled into the parking lot of the office and saw Drew's car. What the …?

I grabbed my bags and walked over to his car and tapped on his window, "Drew, what are you doing here?"

"I came to talk to you, because you've been ignoring my calls."

"Uh, there's a reason for that."

"April, please just listen to me. I'm sorry for overstepping my boundaries with you, it's just I thought we had something."

"We did but it was just sex, or so I thought. It looks like you've gotten your feelings involved and that was not part of the deal, you're married."

"I know, but I love you."

"Whoa! What part of you're married are you not comprehending?"

"I'm just being honest. You know what I deal with at home, but you make loving you easy. I want you."

"This conversation is over. I made the mistake of sleeping with my friend's husband. If you think I am going to take you after you leave her only to leave me for someone else, you can think again. Go home or work or wherever you are going and leave me alone."

"April--"

"Drew, please leave my job.

"Can we talk later?"

"No!" I said as I turned to walk into the building. The last thing I needed today was some extra drama.

I was in my office most of the day because I had so much paperwork to finish for this huge divorce case the firm was working on. It was so tedious that I could feel a migraine coming. I was sitting at my desk rubbing my temples when Gerald knocked on the door.

"Hey, you ok?" He said walking in.

"Yea, I just have a headache. I've been working on the Dawkins divorce all day."

"Well, dealing with that will cause that. Do you need me to get you anything from the medicine cabinet?"

"No, I have some ibuprofen in my purse that I'm about to take."

"Do you want a rain check for tonight?"

"No, I'll be good by then. What do you want to do?"

"I was thinking of dinner and a movie, at my place if you're comfortable with that. I promise, I won't take advantage of you."

"You won't? Then I'm not coming." I laughed. "But, I'm cool with that. What time?"

"How about 8?" He asked writing his address down on a sticky note.

"Cool, do I need to bring anything?"

"Just your appetite."

"I definitely will. I'll see you then."

I sat back in my chair smiling as I anticipated the dinner tonight. It made me think of the good times with Warren, my ex-fiancé, but then the night of catching him in bed with his co-worker erased all that.

I was out of town and flew back a night early to surprise him. I made it to the condo we shared and I saw his car in the driveway. I left my bags in the car so that I could slide in without making a lot of noise. I opened the door and heard the TV on in the living room, but he was not on the couch. I dropped my keys on the table as I made my way to the bedroom unbuttoning my jacket. I heard him laugh, but thinking he was on the phone, I pushed the bedroom door open only to find him being tickled by the lips of some chick.

"What the fuck!" I yelled.

"April, baby!" He screamed as I grabbed her by her hair. "Wait, it's not what you think." He was saying while he was running behind me as I drug her ass out of my house. I opened the door and pushed her out on the porch. I slammed the door and turned around and punched him dead in the mouth.

"It's not what I think? Couldn't you come up with something better than that?" I asked kicking him between the legs. "You got the nerve to be screwing some bitch in my house, in my bed and it's not what I think!"

"April, please let me explain." He said as I kicked him again.

"You don't have a damn thing to explain to me. You need to have your stuff out of here by the time I get back." I said as I was getting my keys. I walked out of the door to find her hiding on the porch. I didn't even look her way because although she had some fault, I blamed him the most.

"April! Hello ... April, did you hear me?"

"Shay? What did you say?"

"I was asking if you had the briefs that Mr. Solomon needs for court on Monday."

"Yea, I'm sorry. I didn't even hear you come in." I said getting the file. "Here it is."

"I know, I could tell that you were deep in thought. Thinking about your new boo?"

"I don't have a new boo."

"Girl, all these skanks are talking about you and Gerald."

"Well, let them talk because I could care less. Is there anything else you needed because I'm about to leave for the weekend?"

"No, this is it. Have a great weekend."

"Thanks you too."

I left the office and stopped to get my nails done before going home to shower and change. I'm kind of nervous about going to Gerald's house because it's been 2 years since I've really liked a man. I shower, comb my hair and put on a little makeup. I decide on some skinny jeans, a cute top with a blazer and stilettos. I did one last glance in the mirror before I turned out the lights, grabbed my purse and headed for the door.

I pulled into Gerald's driveway and I sat there for a few minutes to get my mind right. Come on April, he's just a man girl, get it together. I turned off the car, grabbed my purse and headed towards the front door. Before I could ring the doorbell, he opened the door with a huge smile.

"What are you smiling about?" I asked him.

"I'm glad you came. I thought you weren't going to come in for a minute."

"You saw me sitting out here, I'm so embarrassed."

"Don't be, come on in"

I walked in and he gave me a hug and a kiss on my cheek. "It smells good in here, what are you cooking?"

"Some tilapia, green beans and baked potatoes. Is that, ok because if not, we can order out?"

"No, that sounds great and I am starving."

"Well follow me to the dining room and I'll get you a glass of wine."

We sat down for dinner and it was great because he is a good cook. I didn't want to seem greedy, but I didn't eat lunch, so the hell with trying to be cute.

"I have a pound cake that my mom made, you want a slice?"

"No, not right now, I'm stuffed. You are a great cook."

"Thank you. Why don't we move to the den to find a movie, unless you're ready to go?"

"No, a movie would be great."

"What's your preference?"

"Scary or comedy," I replied.

"Well let's see," he said turning on Netflix.

He picked a scary movie called Devil. I think he did it so I would sit close to him but I didn't mind because he smelled great. By the time the movie went off it was almost midnight.

"That was a good movie." I said yawning. When I turned to him, he kissed me and before I could stop him I found myself enjoying it. I had to catch myself and push back.

"I'm sorry, but I've been wanting to do that ever since you walked in."

"Why did you wait?"

"Because I was trying to be a gentleman."

"Aw, that's so sweet," I laughed.

"You're laughing at me?" He said grabbing and tickling me.

"Ok, Ok! I'm sorry," I said out of breath.

He kissed me again and again, I had to stop him. I didn't want to sleep with him on the first date because I didn't want this to just be about sex.

"MMmmm, you taste so good." He moaned.

"And so do you but, um, we have to stop." I said. "Please don't get me wrong, your lips feel great, but I don't want to start this off with sex on the first date."

"I agree with you."

I laughed.

"What's funny?" He asked.

"It's not that I don't believe you, but you're a man."

"April, listen to me. I don't want this to be a booty call because I like you, I really like you and I really want to see where this goes."

I smiled because he was saying all the right things and as bad as I wanted to sleep with him, I couldn't.

"Thank you for being honest because I want to also see where this goes. I'm going to go before this goes too far." I said getting up. "Thank you for a great night, I really have enjoyed myself." I said giving him a hug.

"So did I and I hope this is a first of many dates to come?"

"Oh, it is." I said as he walked me to the car.

He kissed me and opened my door. "Call me when you make it home."

I got in my car smiling. Thank you God for a wonderful night. Whew I hope this works out. I mumbled as I pulled out of his driveway. I made it home, still smiling but that was quickly gone when I got to the front door. "Drew, what in the hell are you doing here?'

"Where have you been April?"

"Didn't we already have this conversation? You don't have the right to question me, go home to Stephanie, your wife!" I said moving pass him to unlock the door when he grabbed my arm.

"What are you doing? Let me go!" I said pushing him. "You got the nerve to grab me. Seriously Drew? You need to leave my motherfucking house and lose my number." I said as I slammed the door in his face.

Chapter 9
Meet Eve

I loved hanging out with my friends, but sometimes the drama that comes with it can really drain a person. Thursdays are supposed to be a fun night not a fight night. I just don't understand why Stephanie has to act so bossy, always worrying about everybody else's business, and not her own. I had to even get on her when it came to my personal business.

"And why are you rushing?" Stephanie looked at me.

"Well, unlike you, Miss. Boss Lady, I do have a wedding to plan." I forced my lips into a smile.

"Are you sure that you want to waste all your money on this big and elaborate wedding that you are planning. I mean, hell there's better ways to waste your money then on a wedding that only lasts one day." Stephanie said.

I simply shook my head. "I'm going to keep it Christian, because that's what I am. I can say that I am thankful that God has blessed me with a wonderful and faithful man, so how I spend my money is my business."

"Amen, Eve," April interjected.

"And on that note, I will see y'all at our next hang out." I said as I walked out, heading to my car.

I got home in time enough to call my wedding planner who is also my sister in Christ, Brenda Ward. We were both members of One Love Fellowship Baptist Church. Her jet black hair was always in a different style. One day she would have it short and curly, and then the next day it would be long and wavy. For me, I don't have to worry about changing my hair because I love having and wearing my hair natural just like God intended it to be. At forty-four, Brenda was energetic, and always busy. She was our church administrative and event planner. So when I needed an event planned, I knew just who to call.

"Hey, Sister Brenda. I'm calling to see how everything is coming along with the wedding plans." My eyes scanned the photo that was on the end table. I picked up the photo and smiled, knowing that I'm about to be a married a woman.

It was a photo taken of Jared and me on a vacation trip to Florida last year. It was also the same day he asked me to marry him. I couldn't believe my prayers were answered when this 6ft, mocha complexion man-candy wanted to wife me. It was at his work place where we first met two and half years ago. I was thinking about taking a business class so that I could apply for the administrative assistant position that was to come open next year at my church.

Once I was done registering, I decided to get something to eat. I went to get a bag of chips out of a vending machine, but the bag was stuck. He came over and somehow shook the machine, causing my bag to drop down. We chatted and reluctantly I gave him my number. I let him know that I am a woman of faith and I don't believe in taking the top off my cookie jar for anyone unless he's planning on putting a ring on this. Once he understood my position, I didn't have any problem with him pushing up on me or throwing sex in face. I was glad to see that he respected my wishes on sex and more important he respected me as a woman. Ever since then we have been together, and I couldn't be happier.

Now between Jared being a basketball coach at the University of Washington State College and me splitting my time as a Sunday school English teacher, and a high school English teacher it was rough, but we were able to work it out so we could spend more time together.

"So far everything is going okay, but we still need a cake, flowers and a venue." Brenda said, breaking me out of my thoughts.

"I was waiting on Jared to come with me to pick out a cake and venue. You know his schedule is crazy right now."

"Well, what about the color scheme, are we still sticking with blue and pink? I will also need to know what type of budget we are working with." Brenda asked.

"Yes, we're going to stick with those colors that I gave you. I know Jared likes blue and I like pink. I really don't care about a budget, just as long as I don't go bankrupt. I've been saving up for this my whole life, and I believe whatever else I need I know God will provide the rest." I casually placed the photo back on the end table.

"You know Sisters Janice, Vicky and I are still talking about that dress you picked out. I told Vicky, if this girl don't get that dress then I'm going to have to get it just in case I need to dump hubby and find someone else to marry." Brenda chuckled.

"Brenda, you are so crazy, you know Brother Carl loves you." I had to laugh. "I fell in love with that dress as soon as I laid my eyes on it. I knew I just had to have it and I didn't care how much it cost."

"Yeah, until we got to the cash register and she told you it was fifteen hundred dollars. Will that be paper or plastic? I thought you was going to faint." Brenda began laughing hysterically.

"Well, lucky for me, I was prepared. I still have my dress in the same clear plastic bag. I'm just waiting on that special day to come so I can finally put it on. One things for sure, He knows how to answer our prayers, and all you have to do is have faith in Him."

"Amen, amen, yes He will. Let's meet up tomorrow and talk more."

"That would be great, Sister Brenda. Let's meet around ten in the morning. We'll get some coffee or something." I replied.

"Okay, I'll call you tomorrow then."

I went into the master bedroom of my three bedroom bungalow home. I looked in my closet, admiring my beautiful white wedding dress. It was a stunning combination of modest, sleek and sexy. The design of the dress accented my dark, slim athletic frame. The straps were made out of pink Swarovski crystals giving it that bling appeal. This was the perfect dress that screamed take me and so I did. I couldn't wait to gracefully walk down the aisle with all eyes on me wearing this fabulous gown. I could stare all day at my ultimate dream dress, but I knew I had more important business to attend to tomorrow.

I just hope Jared will do his part and put aside some time so we can look at or at least shop around for some cakes and venues.

Chapter 10
The Next day

The next morning, I rose to the warm sun glaring in my face and the morning breeze filling my room with the lovely scent of lily flowers that sat on my night stand. Today was all about meeting with Brenda and discussing everything wedding related.

I wonder if Jared called me while I was asleep, I thought as I got up to get ready. I made my way to the bathroom, jumped in the shower, and just let the warm water cascade all over my body. I could feel all the stress and tension melting away. I became more vibrant, happy and energetic.

I wore a navy blue skirt with a white blouse and blue and white scarf that draped perfectly over my shoulders. I went into the kitchen to check the time and to make a few calls. It was nine-fifty, so I picked up my cell phone off the counter and speed-dial Jared's number. His phone instantly went to voice mail.

Why does he have his phone off? He's probably still sleeping. I just shrugged my shoulders and continued to place another call.

"Hey, girl, where you at?" I asked once Brenda answered the phone.

"I just pulled in front of the house. You can come on out."

"Alright, I'm on my way." I ended my call, grabbed my house keys, and purse.

"Good morning," Brenda said cheerfully as I got into the car.

"Good morning to you, too." I closed the door and rolled down the window. "Today is such a beautiful day today."

"I can't wait to sit down and have me some coffee." Brenda said as we pulled off.

"Yea, we know how you love to have your coffee." I responded with a smile.

"Hey, there's Starbucks right up ahead if you want to stop there?" Brenda pointed out the window to the coffee shop ahead. "Or do you want to stop at Tim Horton?"

"Let's just go to Tim Horton since it is close." I pointed out the window to the coffee shop which was a much shorter distance than Starbucks. "It really doesn't make sense to past one coffee place for another. Shoot, coffee is coffee to me, no matter who makes it or where it comes from."

We pulled into Tim Horton's parking lot, while she was doing that I went ahead and checked my cell phone to see if I had any missed calls from Jared or my girlfriends. Just as I thought, no voice messages and no text messages. I quickly closed my phone and placed it back in my purse.

As usual, the place was packed with the morning coffee fiends. We gave our orders at the register and proceeded to a table by the window. Brenda had the French Vanilla Mocha and a Turkey Sausage breakfast sandwich while I had a Mocha Latte and a Flatbread Panini.

"So tell me, how was your date night with your friends?" Brenda took a sip of coffee.

"Girl, it's like being in one of those crazy reality shows." I took a bite of my Panini.

51

"Wow that sounds bad! What happened?" Brenda took another sip of her coffee.

"Well, we were all just having a good time at April's place until the wine got to flowing. It went from laughing and eating to name calling, then the next thing I knew drinks were being thrown."

"Girl, are you serious? What happened to cause it to turn so ugly?"

"Now you know I don't like putting nobody's business out in the street, but these women have got some serious issues. I mean everybody is sleeping with each other's man, husband or whatever else you want to call it depending on who you're referring to."

"I'm telling you, a man will break up any relationship between two women, especially the cheating kind." Brenda said, wagging her finger.

"This time it was Stephanie and Keli. I mean, if it wasn't for Delilah and me stepping in between those two, no telling what might have happen." I finished off my Panini. "All because of man."

"What about Jared…." Brenda started to ask, but I was quick to cut her off.

"And what about Jared?" I got defensive.

"Calm down, Eve, you didn't let me finish. I was just going to say aren't you afraid he might be doing the same?"

"Now, why would I be afraid of Jared?" I folded my arms across my chest. I was clearly pissed.

"I'm talking about him cheating. You know he don't have the same faith as we do and a man without faith is bound to do anything."

"Well, Jared is different." I waved my hands as to dismiss her snooty little comment. "Jared and I love each other. He respects me and cares about my feelings. Trust me, he would never do anything to hurt me, and you want to know why…it's because he loves me and understands me."

"I just hope it all works out for the best. I just don't want you to get hurt."

I waved my fingers in her face. "Ya see, that's where you are wrong. I am a strong believer in my faith and whatever is done in the dark will come to light." I turned my head to the window, smiling at the bright warm sun. "Right now, all I see is the light."

"Well, I'm not here to judge you and I do love you, but at the same time I don't want to see you get hurt."

I looked at her. "Well, I'm not!" I snapped. "Anyway, I thought we supposed to be talking about the plans for my wedding."

"You're right, Eve, you're right. So did you and Jared pick out a cake and a location yet?"

"No, not yet. I'll give him a call later on today."

Brenda reached in her large purse and pulled out a notebook and a pencil. "Okay, then what about the guest list? And we still need a venue so we can do the wedding rehearsal. Oh, let's not forget about the flowers, and a dinner rehearsal."

"I see you came prepared with your notebook and pencil. I didn't know I need to learn how to eat." I chuckled. "I don't see any point in having any type of rehearsals."

"Well, I can tell you there's more into planning a wedding than just picking out a dress and a ring." Brenda sat her pencil down then picked up her cup.

"I still don't know why I need to have a rehearsal? Why can't I just tell everyone to show up on time and be on your best behavior?"

"Because, Eve, you have to have a wedding rehearsal so everyone will know how to walk and where to stand. Its best, in fact, it's very important to have a wedding rehearsal to make sure everything and everyone is in order." Brenda glared at me from the top of her cup before she took another sip. "I do mean everyone since you just explained how your friends conducted themselves yesterday."

I smiled wanly, because I knew she was right. "I see."

She placed her cup down and picked up her pencil. "We have to do this because we need to make sure all the problems are resolved and all parties are present for the wedding. That's if you want to have a perfect wedding."

"How long does this wedding rehearsal take and where?" I looked at my fingers, still admiring my beautiful diamond engagement ring.

I had to admit, I didn't know much about planning a wedding. Maybe I should've gone with my first mind and just let the court system married us.

"I can tell you for a fact that a normal rehearsal usually takes maybe one or two days before the wedding, but it also depends on the number of bridesmaids, groomsman and the maid of honor. And to answer the second part of your question about the where, well that's also where you have the ceremony. That's why I need to know if you have any venues in mind."

"Well, okay then. I got you and I'm going to work on that right now," I agreed, but I was distracted. "Look, I need to use the ladies' room real quick. I'll be right back." I excused myself, and abruptly got up from the table.

Just as soon as I got into the restroom, I pulled out my cell phone and placed another called to Jared.

And once again it went straight to voice mail. This time I left a message.

Jared, I need you to call me so we can go look at some cakes. We also need to pick a venue, get a list of my bridesmaids your groomsman, and not to mention we need to set up a date and time to have a wedding rehearsal. Oh, and by the way, where are you? It's going on noon, and why is your phone turned off? Call me as soon as you get this message, and I don't care what time it is.

I quickly closed my phone and returned to my table.

"Are you okay?" Brenda asked me as soon as I was seated.

"Everything is fine." I smiled to hide my uneasiness.

"Well, maybe we should pick this up another time. I can check out some venues for you." Brenda said as she put her items back into her large purse.

"That'll be great. Thanks for today."

We headed to her car, and I must say the drive home was very awkward. I was sensing that maybe Sister Brenda didn't think I was ready for this grand wedding. I must admit I did felt a little naïve. I was relieved when we finally pulled in front of my home.

"Don't forget, Eve, I need to know how many people are in your parties. We also need to schedule a rehearsal date, too."

"No problem, I'm right on it." I assured her before she drove off.

It was still early, so I decided to stop by the high school. There were papers that needed to be graded and a lesson plan that needed to be made. I pulled into the reserved space that was mark staff parking. I entered the office, which had a few staff members gossiping as usually. I went straight ahead into my office and decided to make one more last attempt to called Jared.

"Hey, baby, I was just about to call you." I was shocked when he finally answered the phone.

"What took you so long to answer your phone? Why was your phone off? Did you get any of my messages? And where are you at anyway?"

"Girl, slow your role. Breathe! Dang, what's with all these question? I told you that my day was going to be busy."

"So you couldn't take a few second out of your busy schedule to call me?"

"I'm calling you now ain't I?" Jared returned.

"You know you are too smart for your own good." I sat back comfortably in my chair. "So what did you do this morning that got you so busy for you not to return my calls?"

"I um, I had to pick up my tux."

"Oh, really? I thought you had already gotten your tux last week."

"I had class, too. I told you I had a busy day."

"So which is it, did you go pick up your tux or did you have class?" I was a little confused.

"I did both actually. The tux was too small, so I had to get it adjusted. I was in there for two hours before I had to go to work."

"So where are you now?"

"Out."

"Just out! Out where?"

"Driving," He paused. "Why? Is everything okay?"

"I want to know if you can swing by the house. We need to talk about this wedding."

"Sure, just give me forty minutes."

"Love you." I ended my called quickly so I could make it home in time enough before Jared showed up.

I changed into a pair of black jeans, white shirt, and a pair of pink house slippers. I wanted to feel relaxed and comfortable around Jared. I was in the kitchen when I heard the doorbell ring. I was happy to see my baby standing there with a 16oz takeout cup from my favorite restaurant. I quickly grabbed it, opened the lid and saw that he gotten my favorite chocolate covered strawberry milkshake from Steak-N-Shake.

"Thanks, babe." I went back into the kitchen with Jared following closely behind me.

"Just wanted to show my love that's all." He walked up behind me and kissed me on my neck.

"You know me too well." I love how I always melted in his arms when he's around. "How was work?"

"I had to show them guys how to do certain moves on the court."

I sat my cup on the counter and turned toward him. "You're the coach. I don't understand why you have to do all that running and jumping around anyway."

"Yea, I know. I want them to see that I can do more than just coach." He smiled at me and continued. "You didn't tell me how your ladies' night out went." He draped his arm over my shoulder and kissed me on my forehead.

"You know it's always the same thing, we talk, laugh, argue and storm out until we meet again." I replied like it was the norm.

"So, what got you blowing up my phone and leaving threatening messages?"

"I did not threaten you in any type of way. I needed to talk to you about our wedding."

"I can't wait to be married to you. I especially can't wait till our wedding night so I can pop that cherry." Jared said as he kissed me lightly on my lips.

I took a small step back. "Seriously, Jared, we need to go shopping for a cake, flowers, venue and not to mention we need a guest list of how many people we're going to invite."

"Baby, I am serious." He put his hands on the bulge that was growing between his legs.

"Jared, come on now. I have a lot on my plate, and I can't handle this without your help." I was getting upset because he knows how much this wedding means to me.

"Come here," he pulled me close to him and kissed me lightly on my lips. This time I didn't pull away. "Just give me a date and time and we can look at some cakes. I'll let you decided on the venue and location."

"Okay, but we still have to do a wedding rehearsal. I'm going to have my sorority sisters as my bridesmaids."

"Really?" Jared smirked. "You sure you want Stephanie, April, Delilah, Keli and Heaven all in the same room? I mean, they are wild bunch." He chuckled.

"Everybody has a certain characteristic, that's what makes them all so special."

"Special case." Jared mumbled.

"What did you say?"

"I said yes they are special." Jared smiled.

"Now, I'm still not done about this wedding. I know we decided on the pink and blue colors, but I think that we should add another color. We also have to go over the type of flowers we're going to have, too. What kind of flowers do you like?"

"Eve, I don't care what type of cake and I sure as hell don't care about any dumb flowers. We can just get a store cake and some plastic flowers for all I care. The most important thing I care about is us walking down that aisle together and you becoming my wife."

I instantly blushed and planted a kiss on his lips. "See, that's why I love you so much. You're such a good man to me, so loving, caring, and understanding in more ways than one."

"Yes, I am indeed a good man, and I can say that I am glad to have you as my woman, wife and soon to be mother to our nine children."

"NINE!" I looked at him like he was crazy.

He busted out laughing. "I mean you're still young. You're only thirty-one. Your body can handle it."

"Whatever." I playfully rolled my eyes.

"Girl, I'm only playing with you. I do want at least two."

"Do you want something to eat while you're here?" I have some left over steak and mashed potato that I can heat up real quick."

Jared sat at the table. "Sure, that would be great. So when you want to do all this cake shopping?"

I turned around to get the leftovers out of the frig and placed the container in the microwave. "Probably this weekend. I have to check my schedule."

"Well, just call me."

As soon as the timer went off, I took the hot container out and set it in front of Jared. I gave him a fork out of the kitchen drawer and a grape juice out of the frig.

"I tried calling you earlier today and yesterday, but you still didn't return any of my calls." I stood in front of him waiting on a logical answer.

"Are you still going to keep throwing that back in my face? I told you that I had a busy day. Now, can we please give it a rest because I'm trying to enjoy my food."

"I just need you to keep your phone on so when I need you I can contact you. The wedding is right around the corner, Jared, and we still don't have a venue or a guest list. Then my wedding planner told me that we have to do a rehearsal."

"Eve, babe, I'm really not in the mood to argue right now. This wedding has got you acting like a Bridezilla."

"First of all, I'm not trying to argue, I'm trying to get my point across."

"Okay, you got your point across loud and clear, so now can we just drop it before you ruin my appetite. "He took a fork full of the steak and potatoes in his mouth.

"Jared, I wish you would stop talking with all that food in your mouth. That is so nasty."

"Yeah, and you like my little nasty behind, too!" He continued on stuffing his face. "I don't know if this wedding got you acting crazy or if it's the fact that you continued to hang out with them friends of yours."

"Those women are my closest friends and I have known them much longer than I have known you."

He looked at me. "So who are you marrying, them or me?"

I didn't have time for Jared's' sense of humor or the fact he was trying to pick an argument with me. I had a lot of things on my mind, too many to count. "Why would you say something as crazy as that!? If you're trying to be funny then it's not working."

"Me, funny and crazy?"

"I didn't say you were crazy. I don't understand why you got to bring my friends into our conversation when it's clearly about you, me and us together and this wedding. Whats with this attitude you're giving off anyway?"

"Baby, I said it before and I'm going to say it again for the last time. You need to calm down because this wedding has gotten you all worked up for no reason. Sometimes I hate talking to you."

"Oh, so how long have you been feeling this way?" I was taken aback.

"Truthfully, "Jared paused, "since I asked you to marry me."

"What!?"

"I'm just saying that ever since I told you to go ahead and start making arrangements, you just went into Bridezilla mode." He began laughing hysterically, but I was not amused.

"I don't see anything funny. I'm serious, Jared. I looked real stupid in front of Sister Brenda when she got to pulling out her notebook and started asking me all these questions."

"Well, that's why I'm here to help you anyway I can." He finished off his meal by gulping down the grape juice. "That was good, babe."

"Glad you liked it. So, anyway, you can start by keeping your phone on and returning my calls and texts whenever I phone you.

"I promised it won't happen again." He smiled.

"I'm sorry for jumping on your case like that. I just got a lot to deal with" I paused to collect my thoughts. "I guess this wedding planning is really stressing me out. I want this wedding to be grand and perfect."

"I don't want you to get all worked up for nothing." He reached over and held my hands. "I'm here for you and I can't wait to spend the rest of my life with you."

"And I can't wait to be your wife." I started rubbing his fingers with my thumbs. I instantly dropped my gazed to his hands. "Jared!"

"What?" He became startled.

"Where's your ring?" I asked, annoyed.

"Ring?" He asked confused.

I shoved his hand in face. "Your wedding ring, Jared?"

"Oh...I," His eyes finally looked at the empty spot where his ring should have been. "That's 'cause I didn't want to lose it while I was showing the class some moves. I thought I told you what I did at work today."

"Well, I still like to see you wearing it though. I want you to keep it on at all times and I don't care what you're doing."

"Fine, no problem," he said as he stood up. "I have an early day tomorrow."

"Do you really have to go?"

"Oh, so you want me to spend the night with you and cuddle you with my love."

"So, you've got jokes now?" I followed him to the front door.

"You just go ahead and set up the date and time to look at some venues and places to look at some cakes."

"You know I will. You just need to keep your phone on and return my calls when I trying to call you." We kissed before I closed the door behind him.

I hurried back into the kitchen, sat down in front of my laptop and pressed the power button. I was on a mission of finding the perfect cake and venue. I did a random search of popular venues in the DC area and came across a fabulous site. The place was called The Diamond Events. It was located on Massachusetts Ave. I clicked on the link and read all about the lovely services that they offered, not to mention they also offered a great menu selection. I clicked on the contact us link, filled out my information and clicked the send button.

The first site I came to for cakes was called The Sweet Life. Once again I filled out the contact form and clicked the send button.

I was satisfied with the progress that I made. Finally! I found the perfect venue and now we get this wedding up and running. I thought to myself as I powered off my laptop.

Chapter 11

Meet Stephanie

"Morning … good morning." I smiled. "And hello to you," I spoke as I passed the junior accountants on our floor, trying to hurry to my office. I was running behind, because my housekeeper/cook/nanny, decided to not get up on time this morning, therefore giving me the added responsibility of making breakfast. Instead of doing my morning regiments to be radiant, I was scrambling eggs for my little ones and I was pissed that my look was thrown together.

"Good morning Mrs. Morrison" another associate said.

"Morning," I continued to greet as I finally approached my office door. My assistant popped up from her seat and rushed in behind me, with my Cranberry juice and bran muffin. I had never become a coffee drinker, never quite acquired a taste for it and Lord forbid if I had to be one of those Divas who couldn't get going unless I had a cup of caffeine in my system. I was fine with OJ, or Apple, or Cranberry in the A.M. and to add, those beverages didn't stain teeth.

"Your tablet has been updated with today's schedule and the only thing that has changed is your one o'clock, with Mr. Burns. His daughter has a recital and he has to be gone by two, so your meeting with him is now at noon."

"Thanks Ryan." I nodded.

She placed my muffin and juice on the coffee table along with my tablet, because that is where I'd end up after checking and replying to the companies emails. I was known as the numbers lady, the problem solver and anytime any one had an issue with numbers it was sent to me. Projects that a couple associates together couldn't figure out, I'd crunch it out in a matter of minutes. I was definitely a benefit to my company and I was proud of myself.

I graduated top of my class, married the sexiest man on the planet and had two of the most beautiful little girls in the world. I lived in Foxhill Village, not only luxurious, but the schools were top notch. Most of the time, I was in my Benz E350 Coupe, but I had two other very exquisite choices of cars to choose from. Even though I wasn't runway model sized, my size ten frame only complimented my already gorgeous features. Naturally beautiful from head to toe, my natural curly locks were now hanging a little past my shoulders and I looked good in everything.

Not conceited, but a bit overly confident. My girls envied me and I knew it, especially Delilah. As I said before, I pay attention to everything and I can see the looks and snarls she makes at me out the corner of my eye when were out together, or at our girls night out. If I had on something new or if I was sporting a new bag or rocking a pair of fly ass shoes, she'd be the last to compliment me, even though I'd compliment her all the time. If I bragged on my girls, she'd wince or roll her eyes and I'd be like, how could you hate on a five and three year old?

I swear, I loved her, but out of all my girls she'd be the one I'd watch. She was the so-called go to friend of my sorority sisters, but not for me. Even though Eve was not as loud as I, we were the closest. What she'd called judging, I'd call critiquing, but again she and I got along the best. Since she didn't judge, she never seem jealous of my fabulousness, so she was my favorite. I mean Heaven and I were good too, because although she wasn't as flashy as I, but she loved and could afford the finer things in life.

If I had an idea for a trip, spa day or what have you, she would always say she was in, not like a couple of my sisters, who I won't name, who always had to check their finances. I'd be like shit, you ladies are college graduates, let me structure your finances so you can allow your money to make money and even though it made sense to me and Heaven, the others thought I was trying to be all up in their financial business, which was totally not true.

"Mrs. Morrison you have a call on line one," Ryan interrupted my morning routine of checking emails and thinking about my girls.

"Good morning, this is Stephanie," I sang in the phone.

"No kiss goodbye this morning."

"Drew, I was running late and plus I told you that I was leaving, why didn't you rush down to kiss me goodbye."

"Because somebody didn't wake me on time."

"Drew, you are a grown ass man. I told you, I'm not your mother. You are lucky I even woke you at all. And I don't know what the fuck it is that you are up to, but this coming home late bullshit is getting out of hand."

"Steph, I told you I've been working late. My case load is like through the roof since I won that big case last year and you know how bad I want to sit on the bench."

"I know Drew, it was my idea, remember? By the time the girls go to college it won't be like it was for us, so yes, you have to become a judge and after that who knows."

"Well let's just focus on me getting on the bench first."

"See that's your problem right there. No ambition."

"I have ambition Steph, I just believe in tackling one thing at a time."

"Well you know I multitask."

"Yes, I know. So you know it's our date night. The girls are going over to my mom's tonight so you and I can have some alone time."

I grabbed my cell phone. "That's tonight?" I keyed in my code and went straight to my calendar.

"Yes, it's tonight Steph. I know you have your calendar right in front of you."

"I do and you are right, we are scheduled for tonight. I guess I better get out of here on time."

"Yes, and I know you won't be late, you're on time for everything."

"That's right. If a person keeps you waiting they don't value your time," I said and glanced at the clock. "Look baby, I gotta go okay. I have a meeting at ten and I have to be done with these emails prior to it."

"Okay, but one question," he asked.

I continued to click the keys on my keyboard as I half listened.

"What color panties are you wearing?"

"Eeeeewwww, Drew I'm hanging up now. You know we are on the company's line."

"So! If someone's listening, they shouldn't be and this is between a husband and wife. I'm not breaking any rules."

The ladies of Delphine Publications

"You are, you're breaking my rules with that crassness, now bye," I hung up. Drew knew that I was too classy to be talking that nasty mess in my office.

I zoomed through a few more emails and grabbed my tablet and Cranberry juice, leaving the muffin behind. Drew had thrown off my schedule by a couple minutes, so the muffin didn't make the cut.

The look of terror on the faces of the juniors when they see me coming is hilarious, but I'd smile and give them a nod every now and then, just to let them know that I do see them. When I really wanted to knock their socks off, I would address them by name and most of the time they'd think they messed up, and I'd laugh inside.

"Henry!" I shouted.

He jumped and dropped the phone. "Yes, ummm, yyyes Mrs. Morrison."

"Keep up the good work," I smiled, giving him a thumbs up and walked away. I know I scared him into having a stiff one and I loved it.

Ryan stopped me before I went back into my office. "Mrs. Morrison, Eve called to remind you that this is your week to host their girls night and even though green is your favorite color, green Jell-O doesn't agree with her stomach, neither does green icing," she read from a post it.

"I have to make an important call, so call her back for me and tell her, I didn't forget, I'm too wise to do that and that the green Jell-O, will only be in the Jell-O shots, and since she doesn't drink, no harm, no foul and lastly, if she don't care for green icing, she can scrape it off," I smiled and winked.

I headed into my office. My house, my food, my favorite color. I said to myself. I made my calls, had my meetings, reprimanded a few of my staff members and then I headed home. I decided to stop at the store first, maybe to find some new lingerie, because as fine as Drew was, I knew I had to turn up the heat.

Yes I said it, he's fine. I knew that I was all of that and a bag of Lay's, but Drew was a sweetheart and I loved him so much because he let me be me. At times, I knew I was being extra, but he'd let me shine and I loved him for that. He was a good husband, the best I've ever had in bed, a brilliant attorney and he was the greatest dad ever. Why was I so controlling, I didn't know. It was in my DNA. My mom was the same with my dad and my grandma was like that with my grandpa. All I knew how to do was give orders and dictate. Luckily back in college, I ended up meeting Drew.

Andrew Keyshaun Morrison was athletic, popular and easy on the eyes. He was tall, tanned brown, had a fresh fade, hazel eyes and a body that wouldn't quit. He used to hang around and I hadn't noticed him until Delilah pointed him out to me.

"There he is," she said.

"There who is?" I asked squinting. He was so far off, I was surprised that she could even see him.

"Over by the black truck."

"Oh, girl, I'm looking way over there."

"Nah, fool, Andrew Morrison, over by Danny's truck."

"Okay I see him."

"I'm going to marry that man," she sighed.

"Ha, does he know that?"

"Not yet," she said and let out a breath of air.

"So why don't you go talk to him."

"Are you crazy, that is Drew, Drew Moe Dee," she said as if I knew that was the word on the street.

"I don't care who he is, if you like him go talk to him, Dee. He ain't all that and he is definitely not too good for my sister," I encouraged her.

"You think I should?" she asked nervously.

"Hell yes. You don't have anything to lose Dee, now go," I nudged her arm.

"Okay," she said and walked over.

Chapter 12

Meet Drew

"Ummm hi." I heard a female voice say and I looked over my shoulder.

"Hello down there," I teased. She was short, but cute and in my face.

"I'm Delilah, Delilah ....," she extended her little hand.

"Hi, I'm Drew Morrison, these are my boys Daniel and Kyle and Mike," I introduced.

"Nice to meet y'all," she said nervously and just stood there.

"Ummm...did you need something, baby?" I asked.

"I ummm, I just wanted to invite you to our party. We are having a party at our sorority house tomorrow and I was wondering if you'd like to come."

"As long as I can bring my boys," I replied.

"Of course. My girls will be there."

"So that's a bet."

"Okay, well see you tomorrow, then."

"Sure," I smiled back at her. She ran off to one of her girlfriends and I saw them jumping together, doing what girls do, I guessed.

"I think she likes you man," Danny said.

"Nan, that ain't even my type," I said being honest.

"Man please, she is hot," Kyle said and tossed me the ball.

"That she is," Mike agreed.

"Nah, she is too skinny for me man. I like hips and ass and she is a bit skinny."

"Well, I'd date her. She is pretty as hell. Pretty brown eyes, long pretty hair, and dawg she is one of them smart bitches."

"Bitches Danny man, didn't we just have this conversation?"

"Man come on, you know I don't mean bitch like that."

"Nigga, yes yo' ass did," Mike yelled and we all laughed.

"Yeah, I did," Danny confessed and I threw the ball into his chest.

We kept laughing and soon went on to class. The next night, I showed up looking fresh with my boys.

"There she go," Mike said when he saw Delilah.

"Damn man I see her," I said. "Chill man."

"Look at all of these sexy ass bitches up in here," Danny said and I didn't even address it. He had a habit of calling women bitches and I couldn't change that.

"Man you ain't never lied," Kyle agreed.

"Come on let's go over, maybe she can introduce to some of these fines ass bitches," Danny said moving before I moved.

"Nah man, then she gon' think I'm interested."

"Come on Drew, take one for the team, shit."

"Aw'igt, aw'igt, but Danny chill on that B word."

"Okay, okay, I'll chill. Ah brotha tryn'a hit, so I'm cool."

We walked over. "Hey Drew, you made it, let me introduce you to my sisters. This is April, Heaven, Keli, Eve and my girl Stephanie disappeared somewhere."

They all spoke and I introduced my boys. Keli, smiled at Mike, Heaven at Kyle and when Eve turned up her nose, Danny knew he'd try to get with April.

We began to party and move around. Delilah was cute and nice, but when her girl Stephanie walked in, I noticed her. She was short, medium brown, medium build, and her legs and thighs were gorgeous. She had on a short denim skirt and a green halter with green accessories. As soon as Delilah went to the ladies room, I slid over to talk to her.

"Stephanie, right?"

"Right," she smiled.

"Are you having fun?"

"Sure, are you?"

"Not really," I said. I really wanted to run while Delilah was in the bathroom.

"What, man this party is off the chain."

"It's not the party, it's your girl."

"My girl," she asked twisting her neck. "What about my girl?"

"Hey, hey, calm down. Put your claws away. I was just going to say, she is cool and all, but I'm not really feeling her."

"Okay, well be a big boy and tell her," she spat.

"I plan to."

"Alright then," she growled and went back to swaying to the music.

"You wanna dance?"

She paused and looked around. "Sure, why not," she said and I took her hand. We went out to the floor and Ms. Stephanie had moves and I was feeling her for real. She turned her back to me and started dancing on me and I placed my hands on her hips, next thing I knew Delilah was in her face.

"What the hell, Steph!"

"What, Dee!" she yelled back.

"How you out here with your ass all up on him like that!"

Their other friends hurried over. "What's going on?"

"Nothing, I'm dancing and Delilah up in my face yelling and shit, like I done girl code damage."

"Dee, what's going on?" April asked.

"Ask this hoe," Delilah yelled pointing at Stephanie.

"Hoe!" Stephanie yelled and lunged at Delilah. We had to keep them apart.

"I got yo' hoe, I got yo' hoe!" Stephanie yelled so loud that it rang in my ear.

"Steph, calm down!" Eve yelled. "What happened?"

"Yes, what in the hell is going on?" Keli demanded.

"As soon as I go to the bathroom, Ms. Stephanie is all up on Drew," she spat.

"AND .... ANNNND!" Stephanie challenged.

"You knew I was with him."

"With him, girl are you crazy, you've known him five seconds, and he ain't with you!" Stephanie snapped and I agreed.

"Yeah, I mean I just asked her to dance. You invited me to a party. I didn't come to be with you," I said and Delilah stormed out.

"April go talk to her," Eve instructed.

"Steph, why'd you do that?" Eve asked. "You knew Dee liked him?"

"Eve, come on listen to me. He asked me to dance, that's it. I'm not trying to hook up. I just danced with the brother."

"Yes, Eve, this is a party. Stephanie didn't do anything wrong. Delilah is just being a drama queen," Keli said.

"Yes, she is," Eve agreed.

"Thank you, now can I get back to partying. That was so unnecessary. She calling me a hoe and shit, that was crazy Eve and you know it."

"You're right. I'ma go talk to her. Keli, you stay with Steph." Eve walked away and I stood there with Stephanie, Keli and Mike.

"So Mike and I are going to go for a walk, are you good Steph" Keli asked.

I spoke up. "She's good, I got her."

"Okay Drew, I ain't mad at you. I see what you like," she teased. She and Mike walked away.

"So what does she mean by that?" Stephanie asked.

"Come on, let's go for a little walk and I'll explain."

After that we were inseparable. She and Delilah didn't talk for a long time, but eventually with some convincing from the other sisters, Delilah came around. It was all about Stephanie back then, but now, I had committed the lowest act in a marriage. I slept with April. I gave in to the constant flirting and the voice of Satan, telling me that I deserved to be treated better.

April was side lining with comments like, "If I had a man to do that for me, or to give me that. I'd suck the skin off his dick." I'd overhear their girl talk with April always taking up for me or defending me for something. Stephanie didn't know that April would tell me when she thought my gift of choice was cheap or not extravagant enough.

First it started with text messages, like, YOU'RE PRECIOUS WIFE TOLD ME ABOUT YOUR ATTEMPT TO COOK LAST NIGHT AND HOW IT WAS A DISASTER.

I'd text back with, SHE SAID IT WAS DELICIOUS. AND SHE ATE IT.

SIKE, EVERYTIME SHE ASKED FOR MORE WINE, SHE'D GIVE IT TO THE DOGS. SNOWBALL AND HONEY ENJOYED THAT MEAL BOOBOO, LMAO.

WELL AT LEAST SHE PRETENDED TO LIKE IT TO SPARE MY FEELINGS.

LET A MAN COOK FOR ME. EVEN IF I DON'T LIKE IT, I'M GON' LIKE IT, LOL.

Then the text messages got hotter. IS SHE SLEEPING?

YES. Y?

BECAUSE I'M WIDE AWAKE ;-)

SO AM I

CAN I SHOW YOU SOMETHING?

SURE ;-)

YOU PROMISE NOT TO SHOW ANYONE ELSE OR TELL YOUR WIFE?

I PROMISE

DOWNLOAD, I'd hit I and it would be her tits, or her in something sexy. We then went to.

COME OVER

I CAN'T

YOU CAN

NO, STEPH WILL WAKE UP

TELL HER YOU HAVE TO GO BACK TO THE OFFICE

IDK

COME ON DREW, IT'S BEEN THREE MONTHS. I KNOW YOU WANNA FUCK ME!

I DO BUT, I CAN'T COME TONIGHT

DOWNLOAD

OKAY, GIVE ME AN HOUR.

That night, I got to her place and the candles were burning and soft music was playing. She did some things to me that made me feel like a king.

Stephanie was good in bed, don't get me wrong, but April was spontaneous. Stephanie was safe, no finger in the ass, no splashing on her tits, nothing extra and April provided me the extra. Stephanie would suck the shit out of my dick, but wouldn't let me nut in her mouth.

With the right gift, April swallowed. I didn't want to fall for April, hell, I didn't even love April, I just didn't want to be cut off from the pussy. I got ass at home, but it was scheduled ass. I knew what night I was allowed to get it and that's what I hated about my marriage. The scheduled time together was a pain in my ass. Normal people just lived, not planned and Stephanie planned everything to the minute.

She was super smart, very money conscious, a great mother, gorgeous, but she was the boss. I lost my pants a long time ago and I didn't know how to get them back.

"Ummm, that smells divine," Stephanie said when she walked in.

"Hey baby," I said and greeted her with a kiss.

"You are on time and just in time for this gumbo. Taste this." I said and gave her a teaspoon sample of the broth.

"Yummm, Drew that is good. Now I know Rosalina made that before she left," she said and put her briefcase down.

"Busted," I laughed. "She just told me to keep the fire low and stir it every ten minutes."

"Well I'm not mad at her, because some of the stuff you be making Drew, just be all wrong baby."

"I thought you loved my cooking."

"No, I believe I said that I love a man that can cook, but that's not you," we both laughed.

"Well I try," I said and put the spoon down.

"Yes, you do. I'm going to go up and shower and slip into something sexy for you."

"Hold on," I said and started to undo the buttons on my shirt. "I'll join you."

"Drew, you know we don't shower together, that is nasty on so many levels. We shower to clean our bodies."

"I know, but after we get clean we can get dirty again," I said grabbing her from behind and rubbing her breast."

"Ummm, Drew baby, what has gotten into you? You know we don't do it unless it's in the bedroom."

"Stephanie, listen to yourself. For once let yourself go. Let's try something new."

"Let's not," she said.

That pissed me off. "Damn!" I yelled.

"Oh, so we raise our voices at each other now."

"Yes dammit, yes!" I said frustrated. I was tired of the boring ass routine and mad that April was out dating and telling me to go home to my wife like I was nothing to her. I was tired of them both.

"You know what, fuck it Steph!" I yelled

"Andrew Keyshaun Morrison who are you talking to like that!" she yelled back.

"You! Can you for once lose control with me? For me. For once, just let me lead and you follow. For once, just be vulnerable for me, for once act like you need me too."

"I don't need you, Drew."

I stared at her.

"No, Drew that is not what I meant or how I meant it. I mean. You know I love you and I want you, but I don't need you."

"Well, I wish you did." I backed away. I needed to walk out before I said anything more to Stephanie because even though I was hurting, I truly didn't want to hurt her. I was the one who went all of those years letting her dictate everything and now I couldn't just combat her for being the person she had always been. I was the one who had changed. I was the one who needed something other than what she had to offer.

Chapter 13

Stephanie

Girls Night!

"Okay Stephanie, you were wrong, Joe is not my favorite R&B artist, he's yours, I'm an Usher girl, Bllllaaaahhhhh!" Keli yelled and everyone laughed. I was drunk as hell and the more I drank, the stupider I got. I knew all things and paid attention to all things so how did I get that wrong? I knew everything about my girls and I knew Usher was her favorite R&B artist. I had never lost at "How Well Do You Know Me". We've been playing this game forever.

"Wait, wait, wait, I did say Usher, didn't I? I could have sworn I said Usher," I slurred.

"No, you didn't bitch," Delilah said. "Now drink up," she ordered and I took another shot of Patron. I loved it when we did girls night at my house, because I could pass out if I wanted to and the housekeeper would clean up the next day.

"Okay, okay, okay Steph you're up, who do you want to challenge?" Heaven said. I knew she was trying to rush the game so she could get to her pretty boy, Quinton.

"Okay …. Eve," I slurred. "I know you'll tell me the truth," I said and then reached for the bottle. I was on the verge of a breakdown because Drew walked out the night before and never came home. "Tell me, tell mmmmmeeeeee," I slurred and then my eyes watered. "Wherrreeee my husband is?" I then begin to sob.

Everyone went silent. I put my glass down and did something I had never done in my life, told my own business.

I heard the music stop.

"Hey, hey, hey, come here." Keli said. She was sitting closest to me.

"What happened Steph? What's going on?" April asked.

"Yes, what do mean?" Heaven chimed in, but Delilah said nothing.

"Stephanie, talk to us," Eve demanded.

"Drew walked out on me last night and hasn't come home," I cried. "I've been trying to find him all day and I don't know what I'm going do. I messed up y'all. I pushed him away, he was only trying to be nice and spontaneous and make me happy and I pushed him away," I cried even harder.

"Awwww, come on Stephanie, Drew is one of the good ones. He'll be back. He just probably needed some air," Heaven comforted.

"Yes, don't worry Steph, he'll be home," Keli held me tighter.

I cried a little more while they all continued to console me. I knew Delilah could care less that Drew left me, but she threw in an, "it'll be okay."

All the girls left, but Eve. She stayed behind and sat with me. After a long while of crying, I sobered up some.

"I don't know what I'll do without him Eve. I mean as strong as I am, Drew is my earth. He is my heart and without him, I'm not complete."

"And no other man is going to put up with you," Eve teased.

"I know, Eve and last night he told me that he wanted me to need him and I told him that I didn't need him to his face. I lied to him to his face. I need him Eve. This house, those cars, the money, it's nothing without him and I need him.

"Why don't you tell him that?"

"I want to Eve, but I have no idea where he is."

"I'm right here," I heard his voice from behind me. I leaped off the couch and ran into his arms.

"I'm so sorry baby, I'm so, so sorry. I need you Drew, I love you and I'll try to change. It doesn't have to be about me all the time and I'm sorry," I cried. I was so happy to see him that I would have said anything to keep him there with me.

Eve stood. "Well I'm going to head home. I told Jared that I'd be home before midnight and it's after."

"You let him stay over?"

"Yes, he stays over, but still no hanky panky. We don't break any rules."

"Ump," I laughed. I didn't know how she did it.

"I know you're not talking Steph, with all the rules we have to follow up in here," Drew chimed.

I hit him. Eve had heard enough of my business for one night.

"Let me walk Eve out and we can discuss the rules, Mr. Morrison."

He slapped me on my ass and I jumped. I see that my husband needed me to break out of my shell and if I was going to keep him, a little change wouldn't hurt.

"So are you good," Eve asked.

"Now I am. I was afraid I had lost him. Now, Eve it's just us and I can tell you anything because I know you don't judge. I know Drew has been cheating on me. I can tell. I know him like the back of my hand and about four months ago, his routine and demeanor and everything started to change. He started keeping later work hours and he withdraws more cash now than ever. He used to just be a debit card man. I feel like he takes the cash so I can't see his purchases.

"I'm a lot of things, but you know I pay attention and I am smart enough to know what is going on in my marriage. My question to you is, am I wrong for wanting to stay?"

"No you're not."

"But you've always told me something about the bible saying if someone cheats, its adultery and you're supposed to leave."

"No, that isn't what is says. If you find out your spouse has committed an act of adultery, you are now free in God's eyes to leave if you want to leave, but you don't have to. You can forgive them and move on."

"I forgive him Eve, because I know I'm not the easiest person to get along with," I confessed.

"You're not Stephanie and as high minded, stuck up and conceited as you are, you are a good person. You're generous, you give to everyone that you can. You share your wealth with no limits. You volunteer, pick up the check, you offer even if I don't ask. I remember back in college, I had lost my little part-time job and I was barely getting by. Even though I didn't ask, you always came by to visit around dinner time with an extra sandwich or slice of pizza or whatever.

"Your delivery can sometimes be tactless, but for the most part you mean well. Under all that fabulousness, there's a heart and that is why I allow you to still be in my circle. You are not an evil person, Stephanie. My point is, no matter how you've been, don't let him get away with cheating on you. We all deserve the best and nothing less."

"You're right. This is why I talk to you, you don't pick and choose, you just suggest the right thing to do."

"Amen," Eve said.

"On that note, I need to head back inside to work things out with Drew."

"You do that honey. Good night, Steph."

I hugged her. "Good night Eve." I watched her get into her car and then headed back inside.

"I'm sorry," Drew said.

"Baby, I am sorry too," I said and we hugged. That was only the beginning and our first step to fix it.

"I want to fix it, Stephanie."

"So do I." I kissed him, that time it was deeply. The house was empty and for the first time, we did it in the family room on the floor and it was amazing.

Chapter 14

Meet Delilah

I couldn't get Stephanie and her fake crocodile tears out of my head from a couple of nights ago. Whine, whine, sniff, sniff about Drew leaving her. As far as I was concerned, that served her stuck up ass right. I mean come on she treated the man like stir fried shit and when she opened her mouth, he faded into her background. It was about damn time he grew some balls and stood up for himself. Either way, both of them could kiss my natural ass. I could care less about their bound to fail marriage. Besides, Stephanie knew out of all people not to expect sympathy from me. It was no secret that I could not stand her, but I tried to keep it civil for the girls. Like they always say, we are bonded by our Sorority Ties I tried to be true to that, but honestly I had my own life to worry about.

Looking at the alarm clock on my night stand, I realized that I had no more time to lie around and day dream. It was time to get out of bed. I had no idea what I was going to wear for work. My closet was stuffed with designer this and that, but I swear, most mornings I felt like throwing on some sweats and T-shirt. It would be faster and fit my early morning mood a whole lot better. But unfortunately for me, I was the Vice President at Savings and Loans Bank, so dressy attire was my only option. Honestly I loved it, but early mornings I always woke up grumpy. However, by the time I jumped in the shower and had my latte, I'm ready to rock!

The ladies of Delphine Publications

Browsing through my massive walk in closet, I tossed several options on my bed before deciding on a black pencil skirt by Calvin Klein, with a red cowl neck tank, supported by a black fitted blazer also by Calvin Klein. The whole outfit would be rounded out with a pair of red classic pumps by Michael Kors. Sweet was my only thought. I was about to head to the shower when Riley, my younger sister, stuck her head inside my door. Riley had been staying with me for a while so that she could save some money for a condo that she wanted to purchase. She was always quiet as a mouse, so most times I would forget that she was even there except for times like these when she would come into my room unannounced.

"How many times do I have to tell you to knock first?" I fussed but I knew it would do no good.

"Dang, Delilah! You need to kill that rule, you know I won't remember." she pouted.

"Riley, that is no excuse. Anyway what's up?"

"Look mom called this morning…" she paused whatever it was she must have guessed I would say no. "Well, she was asking me for money."

I knew it had to be some bull. That woman always needed money. I think she misunderstood, just because I worked at a bank I was not a bank. I shook my head. "I ain't giving her any money so you just call and tell her that."

"I told her that you would say that but she really needs it." Riley tried to come to her defense.

"Does it look like I care? She always needs it. I'm not Savings and Loan, I just work there. I have my own damn bills and the answer is no." I headed into my master bathroom and started

87

the shower. That conversation was done. Had I stood there any longer, Riley would have convinced me to give it to her. Unlike me, she had a soft spot when it came to our mom.

I had two meetings to attend. When I finally made into work after breezing through them both, I headed to my office for some relaxation. But that didn't last long. Debbie, one of my new loan officers, came into my office with a boat load of papers for me to go over and sign. By the time I was done, it was lunch time. Grabbing a sandwich would do me justice. Grabbing the keys to my Silver BMW 535 I decided to head out that is until Larissa my assistant buzzed me.

"Delilah, I know you are on your way out, but Eve is on line one and she really wants to speak with you." Larissa chimed in. She was always in a good mood. That's why I loved having her as my assistant. That way when I came into the office feeling down, she could lift up my spirits.

"Just tell her to call my cell."

"I did, but she says it's going straight your voicemail."

"Shit," I sighed I had forgot to charge it up.

"Okay, go ahead and put her through." I bounced back down in my chair. Lunch would have to wait a few more minutes. As soon as the call came through I spoke. "Hey Eve."

"How's it going? Sorry to catch you at the last minute. I was calling your cell but its dead."

"I know, as usual I forgot to charge it up. I'll plug it up when I get to the car. But what's up?" Although Eve was the closet to Stephanie, I never minded talking with her because she was, for the most part, pleasant.

The ladies of Delphine Publications

"Well, I was calling you and the girls to remind you all about the fitting for your dresses this Saturday. I have a pretty busy schedule this week and I didn't want to forget."

Hmmph! I had already forgotten, but I knew exactly where it would be. "I got it down." I rolled my eyes. Good thing we were on the phone and she could not see the sarcasm on my face. "Betsy Robinson's Bridal Collection at noon." I assured her.

"Good." She sounded relieved that I knew. "Delilah, please be on time. It's going to take some time for all of you to be fitted and decide on a dress." She sounded so nervous and I didn't think it was that big of a deal. It was just a damn dress.

"I will be there Eve, don't worry." I rolled my eyes again. I wanted to scream shut up, but I controlled it.

"Alright, Saturday." Her saying the day again really annoyed me. I told her I had it. Ugh.

"Saturday it is." I repeated. We both hung up. I would be glad when this wedding was over. I did not want to participate. I was happy for Eve and Jared, that was not the issue at all. I did not want to be bothered with Stephanie, with her bossy self. Dealing with her, this was sure to be a disaster. She had a way of pissing people off and I was not the one. The last thing I wanted to do was disrupt Eves' special day but that damn Stephanie could take you there. I would just do my best to ignore her.

Later That Night

After work, I headed over to Jack Daniels Bar and Grill to meet April for drinks. Finally, I would be able to unwind from a long day.

89

"Hey," I spoke to April who, as usual, had beat me there and was already on drink number one.

"What's up chic." She smiled.

"Mentally exhausted." I sat down. "I see you didn't waste any time getting started.

"You better know it. I been dreaming about this Apple Martini since this morning."

"You are such an alcoholic." I joked. The waitress approached our table. "I'll have exactly what she is having." I too could not wait to sip on my drink.

"Coming up." The waitress smiled and headed back towards the bar.

"So did Eve call you today in a panic about Saturday?" April winked and took a sip of her drink. She knew how much I did not want to be in the wedding.

"Yes, and please don't remind me." I smiled.

"Girl I had to tell her to calm down she still has like a long list of shit to do. And she's already in a panic. I mean what the hell! She really has to get a grip." I agreed one hundred percent with her.

"I know right." The waitress sat my drink down on the table after admiring how nice my drink looked, I slowly and carefully took my first sip. The taste was absolutely delicious and it made me feel wonderful from my toes to my fingertips. I was giddy already.

"I guess it hit the spot." April laughed. She could see the relief on my face.

"Yesss." I grinned and immediately went in for another taste. "So how is it going with Gerald?" I was interested to know since she hadn't said much.

The ladies of Delphine Publications

April looked away and kind of scanned the room, then she looked down at her drink then at me. "He's cool." She shook he head. "Like I told you before, he is nice and such a gentleman. And I ain't much use to it, but I try not to show it."

"That's good. You deserve it."

"I just…"she paused. "I don't know, I just want to keep it neutral for now. You know. I want to take my time, no getting serious anytime soon. I don't need him getting any ideas."

I knew how she felt. Thanks to Karl and his crazy disrespectful ways, April now had her guard back up. In the past before Karl, April had always been a playgirl, she never believed in having one man at a time. Mainly, because she just wanted what they could offer, money and all the material things that they could give. But Karl had changed her and she had fallen in love. But she had regretted that after the way he had treated her.

"Look I understand and you are right. There is no need to rush, take your time. If he is not okay with that than you know what has to be done." I never had a problem with being stern. Besides I had never truly been in love. Well there was this one time, but that was long ago and not worth mentioning.

"We went dancing and girl, he has two left feet. Now you know how I like to work the dance floor."

"I guess it's clear what his flaw is." I laughed as I watched April, for about the tenth time, hit ignore on her constantly vibrating cell phone. For the first time, I noticed that she was a bit annoyed by the caller or the call, even though she tried to appear cool.

"Don't tell me Gerald blowing you up already. Damn is he attached?" I sipped my drink.

"Girl, that is not Gerald." April chuckled. "It's the office. I'm supposed to work late tonight, I really don't feel like it though. But I agreed so what the heck." She shrugged. "Anyway, I guess I will get going. Have another Martini and some appetizers on me." April dropped a fifty dollar bill on the table and she was out. She said that she had to work, but something told me she was leaving something out. I wouldn't badger her about it now. I would finish unwinding with another Martini and some hot wings because everybody knows that Jack Daniels have the best.

At home, I entered the kitchen that sat off from the laundry room that's connected to my hallway off from my three car garage. Sitting in my kitchen is Riley and my mom. Clearly, Riley wanted to piss me off. The last person I felt like dealing with after three great Martini's and some delicious hot wings was my mom. I was really in a great mood.

Dropping my Channel bag on the kitchen counter I couldn't find the courage to bite my tongue. "Why are you here, Cynthia?" I looked at my mom. I called her Cynthia because she did not deserve to be called mom. "You know what, it don't even matter. Just get out." I tried to remain as calm as I could.

"She just came…" I cut Riley off.

"Shut up Riley. You know better than to have her in my house!" I yelled at her.

"Delilah, don't be mad at Riley it's not her fault. I begged her to let me come. It's just I haven't seen you in a while. And I wanted to say hi." I hated it when she tried to be nice.

"Cynthia, you have to go and I mean now. Just go. Get out of my house!" I screamed this time. She looked as though she would cry as I eyed her with disdain. As she stood up, so did Riley. They both left the kitchen before I heard the front door close and they were gone.

Upset, I went to my bedroom and laid across my bed. My past quickly came back to me; memories of my drunken mom laid out in the front yard of our home so that everyone could see, her coming to the school on parent teacher night with her eyes dilated and her slurred words. There were many nights that she cursed me and Riley out, calling us bitches then sending us to bed hungry because she spent all the money on liquor. When I got old enough, I had to go out and get a job just so I could feed and clothe myself and Riley. Then she had the nerve to start making me pay fifty dollars a month for living in our own home. Words could not explain the hate I felt for her. Even though she had so called sobered up, I was nowhere near forgiving her. If I never seen her again, it would be too soon.

Chapter 15

Saturday arrived and just as scheduled, I showed up at Betsy Robinson's Bridal to be fitted and pick out dresses for Eve's wedding. April and I rode together so we arrived at the same time. Stephanie, Eve, and Heaven, were already there chatting when we arrived. April and I walked in just as the wine was being brought out. I, for one, was thankful for the drinks. Hopefully that would get me through the day because I swear I wanted to be anywhere but here.

"Hey you, two." Stephanie spoke as if we were her most favorite people in the world, but I knew that grin was fake.

"I'm glad you made it." Eve smiled.

"We told you that we would be here." I looked at Eve.

"And at least y'all arrived on time." I knew Stephanie and she never speaks for nothing. So with her statement I looked around. And to my surprise Keli was the only one missing. Stephanie put a smirk on her face and sipped her drink. She had already gotten started with her normal bullshit.

"Well, either way, let's get started. Help yourself to the wine as the measurements are about to start. And ladies remember you have to watch what you eat over the next couple of weeks. You cannot gain any weight or your measurements today will not matter." Eve spoke as if we were kids. Turning my back and reaching for a glass of wine, I rolled my eyes.

I quickly sucked down my first glass of wine and went for the second, and before long and hour had passed. Then, in walked Keli without saying a word. Stephanie sucked her teeth.

"Hey ladies." Keli smiled from ear to ear as if she were not late.

"Where have you been?" Eve asked.

"I am so sorry Eve." Keli sincerely apologized. "But I had some errands that came up unexpectedly. I tried to get here as fast as I could."

"Well, you're here now, so let's get you fitted. Heaven is almost done so you can go next." Eve was over her being late.

"Humph, maybe I should have finished paying my bills today. That was important." Stephanie says to Eve. Typical her taking shots at Keli. "Eve, what was that you said earlier to all the girls that were here on time about the weight thing?" Stephanie continues as I noticed Keli trying to ignore her comments, but Stephanie just wouldn't let up. "I'm glad I kept my plans scheduled otherwise my life would be a wreck."

You could clearly see the buttons on Keli's face were pushed as she prepared to start her fitting but she couldn't let it go and she turned around to face Stephanie.

"Shut the fuck up, Stephanie." She yelled. "Just shut your stupid damn mouth. So what I was late? I don't owe you a fuckin' apology."

"Wait a minute, chick." Stephanie said, standing up from her seat. "Who do you think you're talking to?"

"I'm talking to you." Keli confirmed, not about to back down.

The seamstress who was about to fit Keli looked on in shock, almost afraid to continue into the room.

"I am leaving because I did not come down here to get embarrassed by Keli's' ratchetness." Heaven said as she got dressed.

"You wait a damn minute, Heaven. Who are you calling ratchet?"

"Did I stutter?" Heaven popped off at Keli.

"Hold up ladies." Eve tried to step in. "Did you all forget why we are here? I'm trying to get married. This is about me, not any of you, so stop being so selfish." Eve teared up.

April and I just sat back and watched the drama unfold. They finally calmed down when Eve spoke up.

"Could you please have them bring out some more glasses of Merlot?" Stephanie asks the seamstress.

"Sure." The seamstress turned and left the room.

Finally, all of the fitting was done and everybody was cool and laughing again. April was having a good time although her phone kept vibrating and she was nursing the ignore button. More and more I wondered what the hell was up with that.

Everyone started looking at dresses and designs. The dresses were being altered to fit whatever style we desired. We were all in agreement as to what we liked but Stephanie had one demand.

"The dress needs to have some form of green in it. It doesn't have to be a lot but at least a little."

"Green," I repeated, looking at Stephanie. "Huh, girl don't nobody want to wear a dress that has green in it. We don't want to look like grass." I gave a sarcastic laugh.

"What's wrong with green? You know all the green I wear is cute." Talk about conceited.

"That may or may not be true." I got smart. "But nothing in this dress says green so why bother." I hunched my shoulders. "Look, I ain't wearing it unless it has some form of green in it." Stephanie flat out refused like a spoiled child.

"Well, obviously you're not going to be in the wedding because you must be drinking stupid juice if you think I'm wearing a dress with green it." I said wanting to be clear.

"Stupid really, Delilah? I get so sick of you low class bitches talking shit to me." Stephanie spat.

"You know what Stephanie, kiss my black ass. April, let's go I ain't sticking around for this shit." Grabbing my Michael Kors bag, I strutted out of Betsy Robinson's shop without looking back. The way I saw it, either I left or I was gone smack the shit out of Stephanie because her chances with me were wearing out.

After leaving the Betsy Robinson's Bridal Connection, April and I went by her crib. Inside, I kicked off my shoes and relaxed on the sofa in the den while April grabbed some glasses and Hennessey from her bar. I made it clear inside the car, before we arrived, that I needed something strong. At this point wine would not do.

"Girl, that whole incident was crazy." April commented as she sat the glasses down and poured me my first shot of Hennessey.

"No, Stephanie is crazy. To this day, I still cannot believe the nerve of that woman. Selfish and conceited to the end then has the nerve to try and jump hood. Bitch." I mouthed then down my shot.

"Well, you let her have it today."

"I'm just so sick of Stephanie with her controlling ass." I was over it. "On another note, what's up with your phone again. I noticed that you were once again ignoring a flood of calls."

"I," I held up my hand and cut April off before she decided to give me another animated story.

"Now wait a minute. Think about what you say because last time you gave me a crappy story about work. This is me you are talkin' to, so I know better."

April looked at me then poured herself back to back shots and downed them both. This had to be deep. I braced myself for the news.

"It's Drew."

All of that and all that comes out of her mouth is the name Drew. Like that was telling me anything. "Okay, Drew but who is that?"

April went to pour herself another shot but I stopped her. At this rate, if she kept that up she would be too wasted to think, let alone talk.

"Drew, as in Stephanie's husband."

My ears must have popped because if I didn't know any better, I would have sworn she said Stephanie's husband. "What you mean Drew? How?" I asked

"Look, it has been going on for a while." I was in total shock. I could not believe what I was hearing. April was sleeping with Drew, of all people. "But I'm tired of him and he is becoming way too attached, as you have witnessed with the phone calls and all."

I shook my head in disbelief, but it all made sense to me now. "But I can't believe you kept this from me." That bothered me because April usually told me everything.

"Trust me, it was killing me that I couldn't tell you. But Drew was nervous at first that Stephanie would find out, so he begged me not to tell anyone. And the gifts he was giving me was worth me keeping my mouth shut." She grinned seductively.

I didn't feel bad for Stephanie one bit. "Humph," I sighed as I crossed my legs. "It would serve her right if she did find out." I felt devious.

"No Delilah, you have to promise not to tell her." April pleaded.

"Oh don't worry, I won't." Pouring myself another shot of Hennessey, I was feeling too good.

Chapter 16

After all these years, I still was spiteful with Drew for choosing Stephanie over me. But what hurt the most was her going along with him. I mean we were Sorority sisters and our ties were supposed to be stronger than that. She betrayed me and for that I would never forgive her. But I always knew that Drew would one day be mine and now the ball was in my court. Drew would have no choice in the matter.

Going for sexy, I threw on a sleeveless dress by Tahari and headed out. I was on a mission. Once I got to Drew's job and told the receptionist who I was, she buzzed me up. To my surprise, he agreed to see me with no problem.

Even though Drew chose Stephanie over me, he could never deny my beauty or my banging Victoria's Secret model body. A blind man would have to admit that I looked good. Drew confirmed my thoughts as I walked in his office. He eyed me from head to toe, but as always he controlled his emotions towards me. Yeah, he thought I looked good but he was not attracted to me. I would never understand that, but at this point it didn't matter.

"Hey, Delilah. This is a pleasant surprise." He smiled and tapped his pen on his desk.

"I was thinking the same thing." I replied with a smirk.

"Well, come on in and have a seat." He invited, but the room felt uninviting. I knew he wondered why was I there. I decided to cut to the chase. Crossing my legs like a lady as I sat down, I was ready.

"I came by to let you know that I know all about you and April." The pen in his hand dropped onto his desk. My eyes never left his, I wanted to see all of his reaction. He tried to look cool but he was nervous as hell.

"So what does this means?" He asked.

"I'm glad you asked. I have a proposition for you. All you have to do to assure my silence is sleep with me."

"What?" Drew played at being hard of hearing.

"You have to sleep with me." I repeated with no shame.

"Delilah, you must be crazy."

"I can assure you that I am not crazy. And this is not a choice, either you do it or I tell Stephanie everything I know. Once girly gets an ear full of this, she will be digging your grave tomorrow." I grinned.

"Do you really believe that?" He had the nerve to challenge me.

"Well, I guess we will find out. Now you can meet me here." I passed him a card with the address to the Hilton Garden downtown and a time.

There was panic all over Drew's handsome face. I'm sure he did not see this coming.

"I won't do it." He said matter-of-factly. But I was a beast and he did not want to try me.

Standing up, I decided that it was time to leave since I had said what I came to say. I knew at this point Drew was not thinking clearly and he was in shock. Lucky for him, I would give him a chance not to try me. Walking to the door, I turned to face him.

"Drew, just think about it." I said before I exited the room. I gave my hips one big thrust as a reminder that he would not be doing this in vain.

Show Time

The day was here and it was game time. I had carefully made all of the necessary plans to carry out this pure act of revenge and for me there was no turning back. I woke up with so much energy that I did a three mile run then had a healthy breakfast at IHOP all alone. Afterwards, I went home and packed all of the things that I needed for my escapade.

On the way, I stopped by CVS. There was one last thing that I needed to pick up and that was an extra toothbrush for Drew. There was no way in the hell that he would touch me with stank breath. I was a hygiene freak and bad breath was my pet peeve. He would have to brush good or I would be the one refusing to sleep with him.

As I approached the checkout, I noticed a familiar face but it was too late because if I had time I would have ducked. I was in a good mood, but I did not feel like speaking.

"Hey Delilah, how is it going?" Jared spoke.

"Everything is okay. How are you?" I asked but could care less. All I wanted was to check out and get on to my destination.

"That's good." Jared smiled. I could tell that he didn't know what else to say, but being the gentleman that he was, he didn't know how to walk away. So I decided to help him. I suddenly noticed how good Jared looked. I had never paid that much attention to him, but damn I almost licked my lips. His biceps were flexing and he had on a grey T-shirt that was fitting him just right. "Delilah," Jared brought me back from my thoughts for minute. I was guilty of drooling. "Ah yeah," I stumbled. "I said it was nice seeing and I guess I'll see you later." "Oh yeah I'm sure especially with the wedding and all." "Yeah." He responded. "Well, I better pay for this." I waved the toothbrush. "Alright bye." I stepped around him and up to the register. I heard him mouth bye. I don't know what was wrong with me, but I was tripping. I shook it off though because I had other shit to do.

Inside the beautiful suite that I had rented, I prepped for my engagement. I put roses all over the king sized bed, chilled the wine on ice and took a hot bubble bath. Pampering myself in the Vanilla body oil, I felt wonderful. Drying myself off I prepared to put on my outfit for the evening. I had hit Victoria's Secret' up for the perfect lingerie. My choice was an Angel Lace Bustier with matching panties. Sliding on my robe to keep my skin moist, I sat down and started on my first glass of Hypnotic. Two hours later, I had become annoyingly aware that Drew was late.

I was not in the business of begging or waiting on anyone. Pouring my third glass and eating my fourth chocolate dipped strawberry, I decided to get dressed and bounce. My plans from this point would be destruction, slow destruction. A devious smile spread across my perfectly shaped lips as I saw it all unfold. Standing up about to head to the bathroom, a knock came at the door.

Looking at the clock, Drew was officially two hours and thirty minutes late so I knew it could not have been him. Then it hit me that I had ordered up room service to arrive about this time. But I was in no mood to eat alone, so I would have them take the order back. Tightening up my robe I opened the door and to my incredulity, it was Drew.

"I'm here."

"You're late, Drew."

Chapter 17

Meet Keli

"I can't stand Stephanie's ass!" I said between clenched teeth as I threw my purse on the front seat. "Who in the hell does she think she is?" Here I was talking to myself like I was crazy until my phone rang to bring me out of my one sided conversation.

"Quinton, to what do I owe this pleasure?" I asked, answering the phone.

"We need to talk," he said.

"About?" I asked.

"Stop playing games Keli. Why are you constantly saying something to Heaven about me?" He asked.

"Are you serious? You called me to ask about my friend that you're sleeping with? Man please, get off my phone."

"We need to talk, where are you?" He asked.

"Minding my business and seeing that you don't belong to me, it's none of yours."

"Keli, ok I'm sorry. I went about this the wrong way. Can I please see you so that we can talk?"

"That's better." I smiled. "I'm headed home."

"I'll be there in 30 minutes."

I hung up the phone with a smile on my face because I knew the real reason he was coming over and it wasn't to talk. I started the car but didn't move because I should call Heaven to let her know what her boo is up to because I'm such a good friend but nah, I'd rather sleep with him first. Hell, she's the one who thinks he can be committed.

I made it to my house and Quinton is already sitting in his car in the driveway. I opened the garage and pulled in.

"Dang, you must really need to talk?" I asked him as I was getting out of the car. "How long have you been here?"

"I was actually in the neighborhood when I called you." He said following me in.

"I bet you were. So, what can I do for you?" I asked, walking into the kitchen and putting my purse on the counter.

"I want to apologize for this whole mess with Heaven." He said sitting on the bar stool. "I didn't know she was your girl."

"So let me ask you this. What did we have?"

"What do you mean?" He asked looking confused.

"What were your intentions with me? Was I just a good sex buddy when you got horny and not good enough for a relationship?"

"No, I just thought we were having fun. I didn't think you wanted a relationship. We slept together the first night we met."

"I know that but if I didn't mean anything then why are you here explaining yourself? You could have easily called and said I met someone and I would have been fine with that." I said.

"I owe you an explanation because we've been kicking it for some time now and it's only fair." He replied.

"Fair?" I laughed. "Are you serious?"

"Yea, why are you saying it like I don't mean it?"

"Fair would have been you telling me instead of having Heaven throw the shit in my face. I get so tired of them acting like

I am beneath them and this was just icing on the cake to know that you'd chosen her over me." I said as my eyes filled with tears.

He got up and walked toward me, "I'm sorry Keli, I didn't know."

"Don't," I said putting up my hands to stop him from grabbing me. "Don't do that. I don't need your pity either. Yea, we are all connected through our Sorority Ties, but that's it. They treat me like I am not educated enough to be around them even though we all graduated together. Yes, my mouth is harsh and I can get ghetto but I am well educated and if they knew how much money I actually made, their mouths would drop." I said as the tears dropped. "I don't deserve this."

"I'm sorry. I didn't mean for any of this to happen. You're right, I should have been honest with you when I met Heaven but I didn't know who she was." He said, wiping my face.

"That's no excuse because you should have told me, again, if whatever it was that we had going on, didn't mean anything." I said pushing him away.

"I fucked up, ok? Can you please forgive me?" He asked kissing me.

"I wonder what your girlfriend would think if she knew you were here putting your tongue down my throat." I asked coming up for air.

"Right now, you're all that matters." He said pushing me against the refrigerator as he pulled my skirt up and inserted 2 fingers into me.

"Hmmm," I moaned as I raised my leg to allow him easier access.

"You smell so good," he breathed into my ear.

"But I taste better," I said pushing him down to the spot I needed him to satisfy. I moaned loudly as he took her into his mouth and I grabbed his head. After a few minutes, he stood up and unbuckled his pants as he entered me with my back still pressed against the refrigerator. He lifted me up enough for me to slide down on him as he positioned himself to do it right.

"Oh," I moaned as I wrapped my arms around his neck and allowed him to do his thang!

"Wrap your legs around me," he said as he grabbed me and walked me over to the couch slowly as his pants were at his knees. He laid me down on my back and spread my legs as he entered me again, harder than before which made me gasp. Oh, I liked it but I wasn't expecting it.

He rocked me into my second orgasm as his face told that he was at the peak of his. "You always feel good." He said falling to the floor.

"I know." I smiled. "You know where the bathroom is, use it and then find the door and let yourself out." I said walking towards my bedroom.

"Wait, you're putting me out? I thought we could order some dinner and catch a movie." He said pulling his pants back up.

"Naw, I'm good but call Heaven, she'll be glad to." I said closing my bedroom door. Shit, I don't have time for this. I only slept with him for my benefit but I was not going to be his booty call while he gave her an actual relationship.

I took a shower and it was only 7pm so I decided to take a nap before hitting the club tonight.

I woke up and the clock on my phone showed 10:12pm, perfect timing. I thought to myself as I threw the covers back to find my "fuckem girl" dress for tonight. I settled for this leopard print dress that stopped right above my knee, and was cut so low in the back that it stopped right below the small of my back. I pulled out a new pair of stiletto heels that fit perfectly. I threw them across the bed as I walked into the bathroom to do my makeup. My hair was short so it didn't take much to maintain. By the time I made it back to the bed, my phone was vibrating from a call from Quinton although his name was programmed as Chris, the name he initially gave me. Not tonight boo. I said pressing ignore.

I finished getting dressed as I sipped on my gin and juice waiting on my car to pull up. I always took a chauffeured car when I went out by myself so that I could get a little tipsy and wouldn't have to drive. I looked down at my phone again as Quinton/Chris or whatever his name is sent me a text.

"Keli, please answer the phone. I'm sorry." It read.

"Yes, you are but it's cool. You do you and I'll continue to do me. Goodnight." I replied back just as my phone vibrated again. I thought it was another text but it was Eve calling.

"What's up, Eve?"

"What did you do to Heaven?" She asked without even saying hello.

"Excuse you? What do you mean? I haven't seen nor talked to her." I said.

"She is here crying her eyes out saying that Quinton wants to break up with her and I know this has your name written all over it. So what did you do?" She asked again.

"First off Eve, you need to check your damn attitude when calling me. Secondly, Heaven is very grown and if she thought I had anything to do with her shabby ass relationship, she should have called me herself instead of having you do her dirty work and third and finally, I haven't done any motherfucking thing to her or her relationship, so to the both of you, kiss my ass!" I said before hanging up just as my doorbell rang alerting me that my car was here. I downed the rest of my drink as I grabbed my clutch purse and garage door opener.

I made it to the club and it was jumping! The bouncer knew me because I was a regular so he waved me right in and I headed straight for the bar. I downed a shot of tequila as soon as the Wobble began to play, so of course I had to run to the floor. After a few dances and being grinded on by a few random men, I made my way to an empty table near the bar because I was starving.

"Hey, can I get you something," the waitress screamed over the crowd.

"Yes, some wings and a gin and orange juice." I screamed back.

"Gotcha," she said walking away.

I checked my phone again and saw 2 more text messages from Quinton which I ignored. I put my clutch in my lap when the waitress returned with my drink.

"Hey, can I also get some water when you come back?" I screamed to her.

She nodded to let me know she heard me and as soon as I got ready to take a drink someone bumped my chair causing some of it to spill on me.

"Dammit," I screamed and looked around. "Jared?"

"Damn, hey Keli, my bad." He said grabbing a napkin from the table. "I'm sorry."

I snatched the napkin from his hand, mad as hell that he made me waste my drink on my cute dress. "Why are you in such a hurry?" I asked, standing up to wipe off my dress.

"Uh, I was headed to the bathroom," he stuttered. "Damn, you look good. What are you doing here?"

"Yea, I just bet you were." I said looking at his lying ass. "I'm grown and single so I can be anywhere I want. The question is what are you doing here? You know how your wife is about clubs." I laughed.

"I ain't married yet," he said fidgeting with his hands. "Can I buy you another drink?" He asked just as the waitress bought my wings.

"Yes, you can since you made me spill most of this one of my dress." I said holding up the glass.

He nodded to the waitress for her to bring me and him another drink as I placed the napkin on my lap to eat. "You are more than welcome to eat me, I mean eat with me." I said.

"No, I'm good but thank you though. Now, what are you doing here by yourself?" He asked.

"Who said I was by myself?" I replied.

"Well excuse me, I just thought--" he said about to get up.

I laughed, "No, I'm kidding. I am here by myself but that's because I like to party and I don't need a crew to do it with. I can have fun on my own." I told him as the waitress came back with our drinks.

"So tell me Jared, how did you end up with stuck up ass Eve?" I asked.

He almost choked on his drink. "Damn, are you always this forthcoming with your questions?" He laughed.

"I am."

"Well, we met about a year ago and she is a good girl." He answered.

"Yea, if you say so, but how is the no sex thing working for you?" I asked taking a sip of my drink.

"Dang Keli, do you have any limits?" He asked.

"Nope, so answer the question."

"I can't lie, it's hard especially when you have women who are willing." He said.

"And a man capable." I said looking him in the eyes.

"It's not like that," he said with a smirk.

"Man, you can cut that bullshit with me. I can look at you and tell that you need sex just as much as me. Admit it, you're freaky as hell, aren't you?"

"I am not about to tell you that so you can go back and tell Eve. I know how you women are."

"First off, don't compare me to those stuck up heifers because I am not your average woman. I can sleep with you tonight and act like we never met tomorrow. I don't tell what happens in my bedroom. Usually the men are the ones who can't keep their mouths closed when it comes to sex." I said putting a wing in my mouth.

"Oh really? Well, it seems to me you've been dealing with the wrong men because real men don't share their candy with just anybody." He said with a smirk.

"Yea, that's what you say, but get some candy that satisfies your sweet tooth and you can't wait to brag to your boys at the gym." I said laughing.

"Now hold up, you mean to tell me that you don't share your good sex stories with one of the girls?"

"Hell no, not those who claim to never do any wrong." I answered when the waitress came back to the table.

"Do you need another drink?" She asked.

"Yes along with a shot of tequila. Jared, do you want another one?"

"Yea," he said, "I'll have what she's having." He said.

"Be right back." The waitress said before walking off.

"Don't try to hang out with me because I am a big girl and I can hold my liquor." I laughed.

"Yea, well we will see won't we?"

We sat and talked for over an hour and after trying to keep up with each other, I was tipsy as hell.

"Come on with your drunk ass," Jared said. "I'll walk you to your car."

"I am not drunk and I didn't drive. I'm about to call for the car to come back." I said grabbing my phone.

"You don't have to do that, I'll drop you off." He said grabbing his keys.

"Oh, hell no! That's the last thing I need is for someone to see me with you then I'll have to whoop Eve. I will be just fine."

"Girl, quit trippin. I ain't worried about someone telling Eve, I am a grown ass man giving her drunken friend a ride home."

"I am not drunk and I got your girl!" I said grabbing his arm. "Do you even remember where I stay?"

"Yes, as a matter of fact I do, smart ass." He said closing the car door.

I must have dozed off because when I opened my eyes we were in my driveway.

"Wake up, Miss I'm Not Drunk." He said laughing.

"Oh shut up. I'm not drunk, I was just resting my eyes." I said pulling my garage door opener from my clutch.

"You didn't bring your keys?" He asked when he opened the door.

"No, because I didn't want to take the chance of losing them or someone taking my purse." I told him walking to the garage.

"Do I need to walk you in?" He asked from behind me.

"No, but if you just want to come in then all you have to do is ask, but I am not responsible for my actions in my drunken state."

"Really? Well, I am a grown man and I am responsible for my actions." He said grabbing the garage door opener and closing the door.

"Do you want something else to drink?" I asked him turning the light on in the kitchen.

"Sure, what do you have?" He asked again walking behind me.

"You need to stop walking behind me because I know you're watching my ass."

"Well, you have it all on display in that tight dress. What's a man to do whose girl is celibate?" He laughed.

"Wait until your wedding day, I suppose."

"Well that's easier said than done especially with you around." He said leaning against the kitchen counter.

"Ok, I am not going there with you." I said grabbing the bottle of tequila, some salt and limes from the refrigerator. "Come on."

"Where are we going?" He asked.

"Uh, to the living room." I said.

I went into the living room and turned my iPod on as he sat on the couch and me on the floor. We talked about my relationship with the other girls, my job and even my hobbies. I was very interested in what he saw in Eve, but I left it alone.

"What the hell?" I said when I heard someone banging on my door. My head was killing me. What time is it? I said out loud.

"7:30."

"What the--" I said when I turned around to see Jared spread out on the other couch. "Who in the hell is it?" I screamed at the door.

"It's Eve. Open the door! Why is Jared's car outside? Open the door Keli!" She screamed.

"Hold the fuck up," I said holding my head. Jared wasn't moving too fast either because he was just as hung over as I was. "Why are you at my house this early in the morning anyway?" I asked her after opening the door.

"Why is my fiancé's car in your driveway?" She asked.

"Why don't you come in and ask him yourself and quit screaming." I told her moving by to let her in.

"Jared, what is going on?" She screamed, walking over to the couch where he was.

"Eve, please stop screaming. It's not what you think." He said sitting up.

"It's not what I think? I think you're lying up in the house of a known home wrecker after doing God only knows what all night. How could you do this?" She screamed.

"The only reason why I am not in your ass right now for calling me out my name, in my house, is because my head is pounding. Nothing happened between Jared and I. You can believe it if you want to or not, I could care less." I walked to the kitchen to get some Ibuprofen. I took 4 standing at the sink and bought 4 for Jared. I walked right passed Eve and handed them to him with a glass of water.

"Eve, baby, please calm down. Nothing happened between me and Keli. I ran into her at the club last night and I bought her home. We had a few drinks while talking and we must have passed out. You can look at us and see nothing happened, we are both fully dressed." Jared said explaining himself.

"Yea, well I still don't trust you around her." She said pointing at me. "She has been known to steal other people's men."

"I don't steal sweetie, I borrow. And for the record, I don't give one flying fuck what you think about me. I didn't make your man come into my home, and if I wanted him I could have easily had him, but we both have respect and love for you. Well, at least I did until a minute ago. I didn't try anything with him. I am so sick of you uppity bitches judging me. Get out of my damn house."

"Hold on Eve, Keli didn't do anything wrong and for you to come into her house and insult her is wrong. If you want to be mad at anyone be mad at me." Jared said standing up.

"Oh my God, are you really going to stand here and defend her?" Eve asked surprised.

"Yes because you're wrong. Nothing happened here last night and I am sorry you had to find me here but I would have told you if you hadn't have come over. I'm sorry Keli for the way you've been treated. Let's go Eve." He said.

I let them out and I went and got in the bed with my dress still on.

Chapter 18
Girl's Night

It had been over a week since I had heard from any of the girls. I really didn't care because I couldn't stand their asses anyway, but it's our scheduled girl's night at my house. Hell, I wouldn't be mad if they didn't show.

I made it home in enough time to chill the wine and of course the tequila. I went for a Mexican theme and had a taco bar set up in the kitchen. Yes, I can cook. I had just turned on some music when the doorbell rang. Lord give me strength. I thought to myself when I opened it to all of the girls.

"Come on in," I motioned for them to come in.

"What's up girl?" Delilah said breaking the tension.

"Nothing new, girl. How are you?" I asked her.

"Oh, nothing new, from me just chilling. What did you cook because I am starving?" She said laughing.

"The food is ready so everyone can eat and drink, if you want." I said turning to walk into the kitchen.

"Keli, can I talk to you?" Eve asked.

"Sure," I answered. "What's up?"

"Can we talk somewhere private?" She asked.

"Yea, we can go to the den." I said walking to the back of the house. "What do you want to talk about?"

"I just wanted to apologize for how I acted the last time I was here. Once Jared sobered up he told me again that nothing happened and I believe him."

"You believed him after I had told you the same thing. Ok, I get it. It's cool. Let's go eat." I said walking out before she had a chance to respond.

The other ladies were talking in the kitchen until I walked in. "Please don't stop on my account, I am sure it was about me." I said grabbing a shot glass.

"I can't do this." Heaven said standing up.

"You can't do what?" I asked after taking my shot.

"I can't sit here and act like everything is cool with us Keli, because it isn't. I know you still want Quinton and you're doing everything in your power to break us up and then when that didn't work you went after Jared. Will you ever get your own man?"

"Damn," Stephanie laughed.

"Heaven, please don't start." April said.

"Why shouldn't I? Y'all are thinking the same thing, you're just too scared to say it when y'all know she is jealous and threatened by us."

I started laughing. "First off, none of you have anything for me to be threatened by or jealous of. Heaven, I don't have to break up something that I don't want. You may want to check your man, boo, because he's the one that won't stop texting me." I said. "Why don't you ask to see his cell phone when you get home?"

"Girl, who will believe your lying ass?" Stephanie said.

"So, you want in on this too, huh? Why don't you go and try your best to keep your husband at home because obviously what you've been doing isn't working. As I recall, you were the one boo hoo crying the last time we got together, right?" I asked.

"Fuck you! You don't know what you're talking about. You wish you had what we have," she yelled.

"And what's that? An unhappy home with children? I'll pass." I smirked.

"Please stop this!" April yelled. "Why can't we get together and have girl's night like we used too? Why does everything have to be so damn complicated? This makes no sense."

"Then why am I the only one to blame? I get blamed for Heaven's relationship when I was the one seeing ole dude first, but I left it alone. Stephanie is always on my ass when I've never done anything to her either. I don't want any of your men and I can tell each one of you this, I am done explaining myself and trying to be something that I am not. My name is Keli Denise Hart and I will not apologize for who I am and the life I live because I do a damn good job doing me."

"Now, that's the way to shut the room down," Delilah said downing a shot. "Look, whoever wants to leave can do so, but I am about to eat."

"Bravo!" Heaven said clapping her hands. "But that little speech doesn't mean shit."

"That's right," Stephanie said grabbing her purse. "Once a hoe always a hoe. Let's go!"

"I think I am going to go, too," Eve said. "We will get together soon to discuss wedding plans.

"You're still going to let her be in the wedding?" Stephanie asked.

"She doesn't have to answer that because I no longer want to be in the wedding. There is no way I want to be around you fake motherfuckers but I do appreciate you all coming." I said as I stood up to fix a plate.

"Keli, girl you are crazy." April said.

"No, but I am tired. Tired of being judged by so called friends. Yea, I've made some mistakes but I don't deserve this, which is why I can't be in the wedding, Eve."

"Wait, you don't have to do that." Eve said.

"Yes, I do for my own sanity. And I won't be a part of anymore girl's nights. I understand the Sorority Ties we are bound by, but I think it's time for me to cut the string."

"Don't do this Keli," Delilah said. "We do love you. This is only sibling rivalry. We are sisters after all."

"Sisters don't treat each other like this. This isn't what we learned when we took our pledge and I am tired of trying to prove who I am. I will be at the wedding but I will not be a part of it."

"I'm sorry we've made you feel like this and I hope you will change your mind. We're going to go." Eve said.

I walked them all to the door before closing and locking it. I went in and cleaned up the kitchen and put up the food for leftovers. As I went to turn out the light, my phone vibrated with an unknown number.

"Hello," I answered.

"Open the door."

"Who is this?" I smiled recognizing his voice.

"Jared. Now let me in."

Chapter 19

It's been three weeks since our last drama filled girl's night out at Keli's house and I've been avoiding everyone since. I don't have any ill will towards anyone but I'm over the whole girl's night out thing. I'm just not feeling it anymore. I feel that with time and age we've all grown apart, so rather than pretending that we're all still cool maybe it's time we cut our loses and move on with our lives. My plan was to let everyone know I wouldn't be participating anymore when we last met, but unfortunately Keli beat me to it. So now I'm trying to figure out a way to tell everyone without looking like I'm doing it because Keli did it.

I'd just arrived to work and as usual Jewels presents me with a mocha-iced coffee and bagel then sits down in a chair in front of my desk.

"You alright Hev?" Hev is the nickname Jewels gave me because she felt Heaven was too formal.

"Yeah I'm good. What's on the books for today?" I asked taking a sip of my coffee.

"Well we have Libby the lizard who refuses to eat, Maggie the guinea pig with a skin condition, and Max, a German Shepard puppy who needs shots. Other than that we have a pretty light schedule today."

"Good it should be a pretty relaxing day then."

"Should be," Jewels agreed.

Jewels stared at me for a minute with a look of concern.

"You sure you're okay, you've been kind of quiet for the past few weeks?"

"Yes I'm fine, just reorganizing my life in my head."

Jewels stared at me for a brief moment then looked at her watch. "Okay, we're gonna talk about that comment when I finish prepping for Libby the Lizard."

Jewels left me with my thoughts, which were shortly interrupted by my cell phone vibrating on my desk. After, looking at my caller ID I quickly rejected the call and headed out front to tend to my first patient.

Here it is three hours later. I'm finishing up with my third patient and in walks Quinton like we're cool or something. I roll my eyes in disbelief and quickly headed to my office.

"If that fool tries to come back to my office tell him I'm busy with a patient," I mumble to Jewels.

"Will do."

An hour later I went back into the waiting room, expecting Quinton to be gone, only to find him seated comfortably, browsing a magazine. He stands up when he sees me.

He looked up. "Heaven can I talk to you for a minute?"

I ignore him and begin straightening up the waiting area before going to lunch.

"Heaven." Quinton calls out, but I still act as if he isn't there. Suddenly he grabs my arm.

"I tried calling you before I came but you sent me to voicemail."

"Because I didn't want to talk to you."

"You can't keep ignoring me. I'm not gonna just go away."

"Yes I can. Now let go of my arm." I jerk away from him then walk to the furthest corner of the room and start stacking magazines. He slowly walks up behind me.

"Look I know I hurt you but you can't keep avoiding the situation. Eventually you're gonna have to talk to me."

I spun around on my heels to face him.

"What situation? We don't have shit to talk about. You chose Keli over me even though you lied and said y'all weren't serious. So tell me exactly what's left to talk about, you've clearly made your choice."

Quinton slides his hands down his face in frustration.

"Heaven breaking up with you was a mistake, I don't want Keli I really want you."

I laughed in his face and he looked at me as if I were crazy.

"Get the fuck outta here with that bullshit you talking. I'd be a damn fool to fall for those rehearsed ass lines." I continued to laugh at his failed attempt to be sincere. "I swear guys like you come a dime a dozen." I waved him off and began to walk towards the front desk only to have him follow behind me like a lost puppy.

"You could at least hear me out instead of acting childish about the situation."

"Bye Quinton."

"Okay I'll just wait in the waiting room until you get off."

"You do that while I call the cops to let them know I have a psychopathic stalker at my job who won't leave me alone. It's either that or get the hell out, you choose." I pointed towards the door.

Quinton raised his hands in the air as if he surrendered. "Alright we'll talk about this later after you calm down."

"There is no later now gone be with Keli and leave me the hell alone."

He finally left, and thankfully without saying another word. I'm tired of hearing all the lies at this point. Honestly, I just want everybody to leave me the hell alone.

I go back into my office to think for a minute only to be interrupted once again by a knock on the door. "Yes?"

Jewels peeks her head inside. "You have a visitor."

"It ain't Quinton again is it? Cuz if so I'ma call the cops on his ass."

"No it's not Quinton."

"Then who is it?"

"It's Stephanie."

I blew out a breath of air in irritation then rubbed my temples. "Okay let her in."

Being the bossy diva that she is, of course she bursts through the door before Jewels could even invite her back. "Dang, couldn't you at least wait for Jewels to come get you."

"No, now what's going on with you?"

"Straight to business huh?"

"Damn right. Now why haven't you been answering any of my calls?"

"Because I didn't feel like being bothered."

"You can't hide from the world by staying in your office Heaven."

"I'm not hiding, just staying away from people for a while."

"Okay, I'm not people. I'm your friend so that shouldn't apply to me. Now grab your jacket we're going out to lunch."

"I don't feel like going anywhere."

"It's not up for debate. Now grab your things so we can go. I'll be waiting out front."

"As you wish mother!" I yelled out behind her as she sashayed out my office. I swear that woman gets on my last nerve sometimes.

Twenty minutes later we're at Olive Garden eating soup and breadsticks.

"So what's going on with you? Are you mad at me?" Stephanie asks as she looks up from her plate.

"Of course not, you haven't done anything to me."

"Then why are you ignoring my calls?"

"Because I didn't want to speak to anyone. I just need some time to think and sort things out."

"What are you trying to sort out?"

"This whole situation with Keli and Quinton."

"You still want him?" Stephanie asks taking a bite off her breadstick.

"No I'm done with his ass. I just don't understand why the two of them didn't tell me from the beginning that they were serious about each other. At least Keli could've told me."

"Honey I seriously doubt that Keli is serious about Quinton. He just wanted to have his cake and eat it too."

"That's all well and good but why lie about it."

"Because that's what some people do. You just learn to see through the bullshit and move on with your life."

"Easier said than done Steph. I really liked this dude and decided to give him a chance despite how I felt about dating. Then he turns around and does the same thing to me the last dude did minus the beatings."

Stephanie put her spoon down and grabbed my hands. "Look I know you went through a lot with your last relationship but you can't keep hiding from life because of it. For about a year now I've sat back and watched you turn guys away because of your past experience and that bothered me. You should never let one man or experience dictate your future. Despite how much of a jerk I feel Quinton is for leading you on, I'm at least happy that he got you dating again. This just means that he wasn't the one so it's time to move on to the next."

"I guess so," I agreed.

"So what's up with the girl's night out this Thursday? It's supposed to be at your house this week," Stephanie asked taking a sip of her drink.

"I actually wanted to talk to you about that...I'm not participating anymore."

Stephanie sat her breadstick down on her plate and stared at me. "Is it because of Keli?"

"No, I just think that most of us have grown apart, which makes our girl's night out nothing but chaos. We don't even enjoy each other's company anymore."

"I can agree with you on that. I know I'm tired of having to put up with Delilah and Keli's shit every time I attend. Sometimes I've considered calling it quits too, but we've been friends for too long to just give up on one another."

"I guess but I just need a break for a while."

"I can understand that." Stephanie sat in thought for a minute. "Okay how about this: me, you, April and Eve can meet up this Thursday at my house instead of inviting everyone. We'll just consider it a friend's night out."

"I don't know Steph. I'm not sure if I feel up to it."

"Okay, I'll see you around 8pm. I'm providing all the snacks and entertainment. I'll even pick you up if I have to."

"You'll just be sitting outside then."

"No I won't. I guess you forgot I have a key so I can come in there and get you."

"You still got that? I thought I took that back."

"You did, but I made an extra copy just in case."

"You know you're crazy right," I laughed.

"Yes and that's why we're friends."

Chapter 20

A New Beginning

The next day, after my conversation with Stephanie, my plate felt a bit lighter. I was no longer bitter about what Keli and Quinton did and was ready to move on and eventually find a man of my own. Considering this, I decided to change up my routine a little. So I got up early to stop by the coffee shop to get Jewels and I some breakfast. After getting dressed I threw on my heels, grabbed my car keys, and headed out the door sporting a bright smile and new attitude.

As I stood in line at the coffee shop waiting to order my food I felt someone tap me on my shoulder. I turned around and came face to face with none other than Quinton. Is this a test Lord? I question as I brace myself for this soon to be awkward encounter.

"What you doing here this early? You usually don't come here till the afternoon," he smiled.

"I figured I'd stop here before going to work to grab me and Jewels some breakfast."

"Well it's a pleasant surprise." Quinton grabs my hand and tries to kiss it but I snatch it away. Then we look at each other awkwardly.

"I think it's my turn to order." I give him a half-hearted smile then walk to the counter to place my order. Afterwards, I stand off to the side and wait to be called and a few minutes later

Quinton joins me. We stand next to each other sharing an awkward silence as I wait to be called.

"So you got any plans for today?"

I slowly turn and look at him. "Why?"

"No reason just asking..."

"No not at the moment."

Suddenly I hear the cashier call out my name to pick up my order and I thank her silently for pulling me away from Quinton. I quickly grab my food, give Quinton a quick wave, and head out the door. Halfway down the street I hear Quinton yelling my name so I turn around and see him jogging towards me. I look at him wanting to laugh at him running like he's in a marathon while wearing a three-piece suit and dress shoes.

"Why are you running?"

"To catch up with you. I thought you could use some company."

"What do you want for real?" I stop walking and stare at him.

"To talk to you."

"Quinton there's nothing to talk about, I understood everything perfectly. You want to be with Keli and I'm fine with that so there's really no need to explain." I begin walking again but he grabs my hand and pulls me back towards him. "What do you want?"

"I got some things I need to get off my chest."

I sigh in frustration and silently wish he'd just go away. "Fine we can talk back at my office."

Once we made it back to the clinic, I had him wait in the waiting area. "Let me check my schedule real quick then I'll have you to come back."

A few minutes later Jewels walked in. "What is he doing here? I gave his ass the look, couldn't avoid giving him the stank face."

"He wants to talk, about what I don't know, but if that's what he needs to do in order to go away then fine."

After giving Jewels her breakfast, we went over the schedule then I had her to call Quinton back to my office.

"Let me know if you need me," Jewels said as she walked out.

A few minutes later Quinton tapped on my door.

"Come on in."

He took a seat in front of my desk then nervously rubbed his hands together.

"So what do you want to talk about?"

"I want to continue seeing you."

"Well that's not an option so come again."

Quinton rubbed his temples and stared at me. "So can we at least be friends? I'm not cool with the way things went down and I really want to make it up to you."

"That sounds nice and all but I'm good."

"Why are you being so difficult, at least respect the fact that I'm trying."

"I appreciate your effort but it's hard to be friends with you after everything that's happened."

"Okay, I made a mistake. Can't you give me another chance?"

"No. You gotta understand how I've been feeling through all this. I really liked you and thought we could possibly be good together until you did me dirty as hell. I understand that you were seeing Keli first but if you were still feeling her you shoulda just told me that instead of leading me on."

"I wasn't trying to lead you on."

"Then what were your intentions?"

"To get to know you but Keli wouldn't back the hell off. She's been coming at me ever since she found out we were dating."

"You must've felt some type of way about her too if you dumped me for her."

Unsure how to respond, Quinton sat silently. "The best I can do is try to make it up to you."

"Well good luck trying, but anyway I gotta get to work so we're gonna have to continue this conversation another time."

"That's cool, thanks for your time."

Quinton grabbed his things and headed out the door, leaving me battling my thoughts once again.

He Got The Hint

It's been three weeks since I last heard from Quinton so I figured he finally gave up. Since we last met I've done a lot of thinking and decided once again that I'm gonna move on with my life and put this whole situation behind me. Lately I've been occupying my time with going to the gym when I'm not at work and I must admit it really helps with the stress I've been feeling.

Today, like every other day, I get ready to head into my office until I see a man running towards me in bloody clothes and a German Shepherd lying in his arms.

"Please help me! I need a vet quick!"

"What happened?" I asked him while looking at the dog to see if he was still breathing.

"He got hit by a car!"

Hearing all the commotion, Jewels came out into the waiting area after we entered the front door. "What's going on?"

"We need to get him to a room quick."

Springing into action, Jewels led the man into one of the exam rooms and began setting up an IV for the dog. I ran to my office, threw on my lab coat, and raced to the back in hopes of saving this poor dog's life.

"Sir I know you're worried but we need you to wait out front. We're going to do everything that we can to save your dog we just need you to be patient and bear with us."

After a bit more convincing the man finally agreed to go to the waiting room and let us do our job. An hour later after running a few tests and x-rays to determine the extent of the dogs injuries I went out front to talk to his owner.

"Sir it appears that your dog's left leg is broken and will need surgery to repair. Now I don't usually do those type of operations in this office but today I will make an exception since he needs immediate care."

"I'd really appreciate it. I don't care what the cost is please just help him.""

"Don't worry sir your dog is going to be fine, but we will need to put him to sleep for this procedure and we're going to need your permission to do it."

"I'm fine with that just help him please."

After having the man sign some paperwork for the surgery I immediately went to work. Three hours later we were done and the German Shepherd was resting comfortably in a kennel.

I went back into the waiting area to assure the man that his dog would be fine and at home in a few days after observation, but when I approached him I noticed something I hadn't noticed before. This man was fine as hell! How did I not see this before? He had caramel skin sported a low haircut with wavy black hair that made him look as if he could be Dominican and black, a very handsome man indeed. He appeared to workout often based on the cuts in his arms under the t-shirt that clung them. I honestly couldn't stop staring at the beautiful creature before me.

"So how is he Doc?"

"He's fine for now. He's in a kennel in the back resting up."

"Thank you so much."

"Anytime. I'm just happy I could help him." I smiled "So how did he get hit?"

The guy looked at me nervously then down at the ground. "Actually I accidentally hit him while driving to work. He ran out into the street before I could stop or change lanes. Everything happened so fast."

He looked at me with a look of defeat on his face.

"I didn't mean to hit him. He isn't even my dog but I couldn't just leave him in the middle of the road like that. I had to help him."

"You did a good thing by bringing him here so don't feel bad. I know you didn't mean to hit him, things like this happen all the time." He smiled showing me two perfect dimples on the side of each cheek. I smiled at him coyly.

"By the way, my name is Miguel Rivera. I never got to introduce myself with all the chaos." He stuck out his hand for me to shake.

"I'm Dr. Heaven Hayes." I smiled as we shook hands.

"That's a beautiful name Heaven."

"Thank you."

Miguel held on to my hand as we stared at each other. "I know you're working and all but do you have any plans for this evening?"

Just as I was about to respond in walks a man with a dozen roses.

"I have a bouquet delivery for Heaven Hayes."

Confused I looked at the man and took the flowers.

"I guess I got my answer," Miguel said as he looked over the flowers.

"No, it's not even like that. I'm single."

"Well someone is interested in you and I can definitely see why," Miguel smiled.

I opened the card to the flowers; of course, they were from Quinton.

I know you're still upset with me but you can't stay mad forever. I would love for us to meet up so we can completely talk things out. Call me!

PS. There are more gifts to come. I won't stop sending them till you talk to me.

Chapter 21

Quinton

I sat the flowers on the front desk and balled up the card and threw it in the trash. He just won't let me move on dammit.

"So is that a no for tonight?" Miguel asked me.

"Definitely not, I would love to go out with you tonight." I took a sticky notepad off the front desk and wrote my number down for him.

"Cool. I'll give you a call around six so we can work out the details. It was nice meeting you."

"It was nice meeting you too Miguel. By the way, what are you going to do about the dog you brought in? Should I call the animal shelter?"

"No, I want to keep him. I'll name him Lucky. If it wasn't for him I never would've met you." I blushed as he agreed to call me later and walked out the door.

After watching him walk away I ran to the back of the office to tell Jewels the good news. After getting off work I raced home to find something to wear on my date. As promised Miguel called me around six and we agreed to meet up at the restaurant by eight.

Once I hopped in the shower, did my hair and makeup, and put on my clothes it was seven-thirty so I snatched my purse off the bed, grabbed my keys, and hurried out the house. When I pulled up to the restaurant Miguel was already waiting for me out front. Timely and he has good taste, I like him already.

"May I help you out your car?" Miguel said opening my car door for me.

"Sure." I smiled.

As we walked in to the restaurant I admired how beautiful it was. Gorgeous artwork adorned the walls and a beautiful waterfall sat off to the side next to the waiting area.

"This is very nice Miguel."

"I thought you'd like it, a beautiful place for a beautiful lady."

Once we were seated the conversation flowed well. I told him about my older sister who I am very close to and about my mother and father who are still married but retired and spend most of their time traveling. I told him that I have no kids but want at least one someday and that I've never been married or even considered it.

Miguel, in turn, told me that he has no children; he was married once but is now divorced. He said that he got married too young and should've waited but he thought he knew what he was doing. He works at his family's construction business, which he now owns and he is really close to his family. Both of us enjoy traveling and anything else fun that doesn't involve clubbing, drinking, or smoking but neither of us mind going to poetry lounges and karaoke bars though he can't sing.

Miguel made me feel like a queen the whole night. Every door we went through he opened for me while gently guiding me through it by putting his hand on the small of my back. Every chair was pulled out for me without me even having to ask and he quickly took the check without even flinching when looking at it. So far Miguel's won my vote. I'd definitely go out with him again.

The next day I arrived at work and immediately began telling Jewels about my date. After telling her all the details it was time for our first appointment to arrive so I agreed to fill her in on the rest of the info later. Two hours after completing the second appointment of the day in walks a man with a basket of Edible Arrangements for me of course. Dammit Quinton just can't get the hint. I opened up the card inside and was delighted to see that it was from Miguel.

I had a wonderful time last night and I look forward to seeing you again. I'll call you later on tonight. Enjoy your gift.

Chapter 22

Miguel

All I could do was smile when I read the card that was until I looked up and saw Quinton walking through the door.

"I see you got my gift, you like it?"

"It's not from you."

Quinton's face scrunched up.

"Who is it from then?"

"Why?"

"Because I wanna know."

"It's none of your damn business Quinton."

I began walking back to my office and he followed behind me.

"So you're not gonna tell me who they're from?"

"No, I don't owe you no explanations."

Quinton grabbed my arm and turned me towards him.

"Don't grab me!"

"Well you need to tell me something."

"I don't need to tell you shit. You need to get out of my office."

"So you moved on that quick?"

"Go question Keli. I ain't your woman." I waved him off and he grabbed my hand. "If you grab me one more time I promise you it won't be pretty for you."

"I didn't come here to argue with you. I just wanted to talk to you."

"Okay what you got to say?"

"Can me, you, and Keli all sit down and talk? We really need to straighten things out."

"I don't care about straightening nothing out. I just want to move on with my life."

"Please just come over to my house with me. I already talked to Keli and she wants to work things out just as much as I do."

I let out a frustrated breath and stared at him.

"Fine, I just want to get this shit over with so both of y'all's asses will leave me the hell alone."

Quinton sat out front in the waiting room until I got off work. Just as I was finishing up my last patient Miguel walked in.

"Hey what are you doing here?" I smiled as he hugged me tightly.

"You left your jacket in my car."

"Seriously, you could've waited to give me that," I laughed

"Honestly, I just wanted to see you."

"I don't have a problem with that."

Miguel hugged me once again and caressed my cheek just as Quinton walked back into the waiting room from the restroom.

"Who the fuck is this?" Quinton walked up with a look of hate on his face.

"Quinton don't start. We are not together."

"I don't care but you ain't gotta flaunt this clown all in my face."

"Man I don't know what your problem is but I ain't gon be too many more clowns."

"Who was talking to you?" Quinton walked up in Miguel's face and I tried to separate them.

"If you gon do something do it." Miguel stared at Quinton unfazed and waiting for him to make the first move.

"Y'all need to take this outside," Jewels yelled walking towards us.

The two men stared each other down a few more seconds then Miguel agreed to leave.

"I don't wanna be messing up your place of business so I'll just see you later baby."

"Ok, I'm sorry about—"

"Don't worry about it. It's not your fault. I'll call you later okay."

"Okay."

Miguel kissed me on the lips, gave Quinton a quick stare down, and walked out the door.

"What the fuck is your problem Quinton? We're not even together."

"I don't care. I ain't bout to let that pretty muthafucka think he gon come up in here and intimidate me."

"You came at him."

"Are you gon come with me or not?" Quinton asked changing the subject.

"I shouldn't after that shit you pulled."

"Look I promise you after today I'll leave you alone."

"Fine, let me grab my purse."

I followed Quinton to his house and waited in the living room for Keli to arrive.

"You want anything to drink?"

"Nah I'm good."

"So when you start talking to ole boy?"

"Let's not go there. I didn't come here to talk about my love life."

"I'm just asking."

"Well just ask again and I'm walking out that door."

A few minutes later we heard a knock at the door so Quinton got up to answer it.

"Hey, you got the money?" Keli asked walking through the door.

"Yeah let me run upstairs and grab it for you."

When she walked in and saw me she scrunched her face up. "What the fuck she doing here?"

"I thought y'all might want to talk."

"About what? I ain't got nothing to say to this bitch."

"All the name calling ain't necessary, your boy invited me over here claiming you wanted to talk, other than that I wouldn't be here," I said ready to punch her in the face

"Well I guess you can leave cuz we ain't got nothing to talk about."

"Keli I understand that we ain't cool like that and I'm fine with that but I'll be damned if I sit here and let you disrespect me. Now the only reason I came here today is because Quinton asked me to but believe me I don't want your man."

"Girl I ain't concerned about him I only came here to get the money he owes me other than that you can have him."

"Yeah right, he told me how you was all up in his face trying to keep him from talking to me and blowing his phone up when we were dating so you ain't gotta pretend like you don't want him."

"Well he lied to you, cuz I don't be calling that fool like that unless I need something."

Quinton came downstairs and joined us in the living room.

"What I miss? Did y'all kiss and make up yet cuz if so I hope I didn't miss it."

"Why you lying to her talking about I was calling you all the time and trying to split y'all up? If anybody was blowing up a phone, you were blowing up mine cuz I definitely ain't been chasing you."

"You were calling me," Quinton said looking nervous.

"Let me see your phone then so I can show her the calls, then we'll see who's lying cuz it sure the hell ain't me."

"Nah I'm not doing all that, you know what it is Keli."

"No I don't Quinton. What is it? Explain it to me." Keli crossed her arms and stared at him.

"I'm just saying I don't need to show nobody my phone."

"Okay, I'll show her mine then." Keli unlocked her phone and scrolled down to all the messages Quinton sent her.

"I'm lying but in damn near all of these messages he's talking about how he don't want you, you ain't his type, and you're desperate. Here go some more where he's practically begging me for sex cuz he said you won't give him none so if anybody's lying he is."

"Where the rest of the messages at Keli? You know it was more to that conversation than what you're showing her."

"Seriously Quinton, do me a favor and don't call me no more. Good luck with his lying ass Heaven cuz you're gonna need it."

Keli stormed out the door and slammed it behind her.

"Why you drag her into this mess if you knew you were lying?"

"I wasn't lying. She's just trying to find a way to keep you from talking to me again."

"Then why would you invite her over to talk to me?"

"For you to see that it ain't me that's the problem, it's her."

"Yeah I hear you."

Quinton ran back upstairs while I walked around the living room browsing at the pictures sitting on his mantel. I then eased over to the desk he had sitting in the corner of the room with his laptop screen up. I pressed the power button figuring the screen fell asleep and up pops a page of email messages sent to Keli asking her to come over and see him. He'd even sent her a number of naked photos and flicks of him fucking other women. 'This is what I want to do to you.' He typed in the message box where he sent the flick. He came back downstairs and it took everything in my power not to punch him in his damn head.

"You lying muthafucka. I fucked up my friendship with Keli for you."

"Why you coming at me like that?"

"You left your computer screen up and I saw all the emails you sent Keli. You are such a piece of shit you lying bastard."

"Why you snooping through my shit?"

"I wasn't snooping through your shit. Your screen was up. Next time maybe you should lock your shit if you don't want nobody looking at it."

"It ain't even what you think Heaven. I was just playing around."

"Do you really think I'm dumb enough to believe that? Just get the hell out of my way so I can go." I bumped past him and grabbed my purse off the couch so I could leave.

"Heaven don't act like you surprised to find out I was fucking other women. Did you really think I was gonna wait on you? Don't no man want a bitch that won't fuck. You a damn fool if you think I was gonna sit around and wait on you to give it up. Especially when I got other bitches that'll give it up in a heartbeat. I ain't gotta beg no hoe for sex especially no stuck up ass bitch like you. Why else you think I kept chillin with Keli, I ain't gotta beg her to fuck she just gets down and do what she gotta do no questions asked."

At that point I couldn't contain my anger any longer I hauled off and kicked that muthafucka so hard between his legs that the next woman better hope and pray that fool can have kids. He buckled over and fell to the floor and I gave him one more kick just for being an asshole.

"I hope you can't use that shit no more you trifling no good ass bastard."

"Fucking bitch," he mumbled as he rolled around on the floor holding his crotch.

"Have a nice life and forget my number," I said as I stepped over him and headed out the door with a smile on my face.

145

This was by far the best day I've had in a long time. There's nothing like sweet revenge.

Chapter 23

The nerve of this motherfucker coming over here and showing out! I mean who the hell does that when you got a whole wife at home? Granted I have been sleeping with Stephanie's husband but I am not and will never be his damn wife. Hell frankly I don't see what Delilah sees in his ass any way, seems like she dodged a bullet if you ask me.

I walk to the bedroom and threw my purse and phone on the bed. Before I could even walk to the bathroom I see the blue light blinking on my phone. I must have a text message. I open the phone up to see who the new text is from and to my unnerving surprise it was Drew.

I am sick of playing these damn games with you April. You trying to treat me like I don't fucking matter...If you don't believe nothing else believe this...this shit is not over!

"What the hell is his problem?" I mumbled as I threw the phone on the bed and walked to the bathroom. Cutting the shower on full blast, grabbing my red satin robe off the back of the door, and watching my clothes decorate the floor.

The water cascading over my body was like standing under hot water at Niagara Falls. Thoughts of Gerald invaded my mind. I began to lather up my towel with the sweet smell of Caress soap and imagined that Gerald was there.

His hands were firmly around my neck switching sides with ease, kissing my lips then my chin, whispering in my ear. My bottom lip became his snack of choice. "Gorgeous you are." I heard the faint words escape his lips while cupping each of my size double D breast. The attention this man was giving each nipple was amazing. His hands slide over my body with ease, his main focus was to please me. Squeezing both my breasts together so he can send shock waves of pleasure through my body was welcoming. Moans escaped my lips, my hands explored his body. His broad shoulders and strong back were flexing as he moved to different parts of my body to taste, smell, and explore.

His tongue trickled down the center by my stomach, where it rested right at the top of my neatly trimmed hairline. One hand on my breast and the other resting my sweet plump hoohaa was like Gerald being with me. I arch my back and spread my pussy lips so the water can hit on my clit. Pulling back the hood slightly, as the water hit it one way I flicked it another. My body began to shake as I felt an orgasm nearing. "Gerald," escaped through my lips, that pink bud was in full effect and ready to let me know it was time to explode. "Oooo shit...oh fuck...this is your pussy baby...oh shit!"

Damn. I felt the warm cream leaving my body as I leaned up against the shower wall and let my body shake uncontrollably. As the last bit of cum was leaving my body; flashes of Gerald's face popped in my head. Sliding my body down until I was now sitting in the tub my head spun, thinking how strong that orgasm was and Gerald was nowhere around. Taking deep breaths I knew after I calmed down and relaxed a little more in the shower that I was going to have to sleep and dream of Gerald.

Chapter 24

It's Morning

Waking up to my phone buzzing like crazy, I thought it was wise to ignore it. Hell, I wasn't even sure who it was but I knew I didn't want any bullshit this morning from anyone. Throwing the cover off of me I was actually eager to get to work and see if Gerald was going to give me the same treatment he has been giving or was he gonna act like we didn't have date night at his house. I was gonna wear my red Donna Karan pencil skirt with the matching red fitted jacket and cream tank shell adorned with six inch red Jimmy Choo.

After getting myself together and doing a once over in the mirror I knew that I was on point as the people say, "I was snatched!" Grabbing my belongings heading out the door, my damn phone starts to ring before I could even get in the car. Everyone knows that I will not answer any calls before I get to work. Hell it's the easiest way to have a bad damn day by someone else pissing you off. I let that caller go to voicemail and thought about my next date with Gerald, hoping that I was brave enough to actually have sex with him and not take it home and have an invisible shower scene with him.

Being a paralegal was great. I got to meet some very tough lawyers, men and women. You had the few around here that thought that they walked on water like almighty GOD himself, and then you had the ones that knew their talent and wanted to help people who needed a lawyer. As soon as I sat in my chair and my butt started to make a home my cell go off again. Shaking my head I knew this was not gonna be a good morning.

"Hey Ma."

"Hey Ma, is that how you answer the phone when I call you?"

"No Ma, it's just I am looking through a lot of papers on my desk that's all."

"Well you know it's been a few weeks since you brought me some groceries and I need more."

"Ma you get a check. I help with as much as I can. Why are you always so short on food? This is making no sense to me at all."

"Gal don't be telling me what do and don't make sense to you. You sitting up there in that fancy office acting like you don't have to help no damn body."

I laid the phone down on the desk not wanting to hear anything else from her. I was really on the verge of cussing her out.

"First off Momma, I love you and actually I don't have to do nothing that I don't want to do. It amazes me how you try and get on my case about what I do or don't do for you and you got a son staying there rent damn free. If it's someone you wanna be mad at, be mad at Derrick, Momma make him get off his ass and pay his way!"

"Oh I see. You just got all the damn answers, Ms. High and Mighty. You know this boy got court trouble with that gal he done gone and had a child with. It's not his fault April, but I see you judging him like always. You just wait until you need someone then you will see what I'm talking about."

I just wanted to scream. What the hell was she talking about? The fact that my brother was a moocher and a weed head never got through to my mom. But as soon as I didn't do whatever it was she needed me to do it was like World War II. It was just no making her happy. Maybe she was upset that she never got to live out her dreams as a singer due to her smoking and seeing my success over the years upset her in some way.

"You know what Ma after I get off work I will stop by your place with some groceries and money."

"Well if you have time, I don't want you breaking your neck to get here. I think I got a can of Spam in the cupboard."

"Eat that then," I mumbled.

"Did you say something baby?"

"No Ma, I'll see you this afternoon. I have to run talk to you later." And before she could utter one damn word, I hung up.

I started looking at some paper work I needed to get done before my day really went to shit. I needed to have these papers ready to go for the partner's next case. My work phone clicked on my personal intercom line. I pressed it not knowing who the hell it could be. "This is April."

"Good morning gorgeous hope you are having a great day so far."

I was grinning extremely hard and still holding the button down before I could even answer. "Good morning but actually in a few minutes it's gonna be noon. What are your plans for lunch?" Not sure on what he was going to say, I held my breath in anticipation.

"I was thinking we could go grab a bite to eat and figure out when and where our next date will be."

"You called at the right time 'cause I am starving. I will grab my purse and meet you down stairs at in the lobby."

"Sounds good, see you in fifteen minutes," Gerald said.

I grabbed my damn purse and slipped my heels back on. I gave the papers to the secretary and told her that one of the partners would be down shortly to get them. Just as I was making my way to the revolving doors Gerald had stepped off the elevator looking like he just stepped out of GQ Magazine.

"Looking good Gerald," I said with a smile.

"Thank you gorgeous. You look wonderful yourself, shall we go eat?"

Gerald extended his hand for me to go first. Through the revolving doors, same as before, the onlookers were turning their noses up and looking at me sideways. When Gerald came through the doors he reached for my hand and we walked to his car. I heard a faint "bitch" come from one of the women in the crowd. All that did was make me smile and walk a little closer to Gerald.

As we got in the car I looked back over to the crowd of onlookers. Yeah y'all asses wish you could trade places with me. Gerald turned and looked at me.

"You good baby?"

"Oh yes, I am just ready to eat."

"I thought I heard your stomach say something."

"I see you got jokes." We both busted into laughter.

Chapter 25

There is nothing like the weekends, I lived for it. You don't have to get up early, no heels and shit, just house shoes, shorts, and t-shirt. Gerald knows he got me thinking about the conversation we had over lunch yesterday. The more he talked, the wetter my pussy got. Damn I couldn't believe it. We ended up going to a little café where they have the best Panini sandwiches. We got more in depth about our past and that's when I found out that his last girlfriend, who he dated a year ago, ended up pregnant but lost the baby.

It was a tragic thing in his life that he says made him realize that he definitely wants kids one day soon. Now me, on the other hand, I am not trying to be nobody's mother at this point in my life. I love dating and coming and going as I damn well please. I am not about to entertain a full-fledged relationship where I give up all of me to have part of him.

The doorbell rang. I looked at the clock to see the time. It was 9:45am. Who the hell is ringing my damn doorbell so early in the morning? I closed my robe tighter over my naked body. But when I looked out the door I didn't see anyone, but there was a small package left on the porch. Picking it up I saw no return address, no name, no nothing. It was as if appeared out of thin air.

Closing the door behind me I sat on the couch and opened the tiny box. It was the size of a Rubik's cube. "Damn this is the tiniest box I have ever seen before in my life." I ripped the paper off and opened it. As I pulled the contents out and examined it, a small card fell to the floor.

It read...your pussy smells so good.

"What the hell is this?" Looking at the red and black silk thong panties immediately made me think of one person and one person only....DREW!

This was starting to get freaky. Even though I told Delilah what I had done, I'm starting to think I should have told Stephanie instead. Sure it would have ruined our friendship, but who cares. I was growing tired of this group anyway. If it wasn't for our bond through our sorority half of us would not even be friends.

I walked to the kitchen to throw the box and the contents in the garbage there was no need of me keeping it. All I could think of after that shit was spending time with Gerald tonight. During our lunch we discussed having another date night at his house. I didn't think it would be so soon, but I was glad that we were going to see each other again tonight. I hope I can actually go through with having sex with him tonight. The thought of sexing him just right and then find out that he got some ratchet ass girl behind closed doors somewhere is nothing I am trying to get involved in.

Thinking about the conversation I had Delilah made me think to call her ass before she does something stupid cause everyone in the group knows she is still bitter at Drew for picking Stephanie.

"Hey Delilah! Girl what's going on with you today?"

"Nothing. Got some plans later on but nothing major, just going to see an old friend that's all."

"Oh okay, I just wanted to again ask you not to say anything about what I told you to anyone, let alone Stephanie. I don't need this thing to become any bigger than it already is and has."

"Girl please ain't nobody thinking about her stuck up ass or her man. I really have other things to do with my time than waste it on a fool of a couple. I am just fine. I don't need a man to validate me and I gets dick whenever I see fit, so April don't concern yourself with this shit your secret is safe with me.

I heard those words come out of Delilah's mouth and instantly regretted telling her anything. Knowing how she feels about Drew, no telling what master plan she was coming up with in that twisted mind of hers.

"Okay, I guess I was tripping."

"Yes girlfriend. You have tripped and slipped all the way overboard if you think I am still thinking of you and that dude. But I would be lying if I said every time I see her face I would be just overjoyed knowing that her husband ain't no better than the rest of these sorry ass men out here. If she knew, which she won't hear it from me, but if she did I bet that would shut her the fuck up. Point, blank, period."

Listening to Delilah rant and rave about her newfound secret about Stephanie's husband was making me sick. I knew I was going to have to deal with what I had done sooner or later but Delilah is having just a little too much fun with this.

"Alright I'll take your word for it and I'm gone from it but if I hear anything or as much as someone signifying, you and I are gonna have an issue."

155

"Girl please, you are putting too much thought in this whole thing. Let it go. But I will say it is amazing how you seem to be on edge about fucking someone else's husband. It's not like any of us really like her stuck up ass anyway. Well, except Eve.

"I just don't want no bullshit that's all. 'Cause if she ever finds out it's gonna be enough shit to last this sorority a lifetime. Oh and by the way, guess who's man I saw kissing another woman?" I knew damn well I shouldn't be saying this shit to Delilah's ass either, but I gotta tell somebody. Hell, she knows my business now, she may as well know someone else's. "Girl I stopped in Starbucks the other day and got me a caramel latte and low and behold I see Jared ass in there kissing another woman. So I snuck and took a pic and let my presence be known before walking out of there."

"Damn girl!" Delilah shouted through the phone.

"I know right! That's why I do what I do because these niggas ain't loyal," April said.

"Sounds like there might not be a wedding after all, especially since that bullshit that took place at the bridal shop. It's not like I wanted to be there in the first damn place."

"Well Delilah, we both gotta keep this under wraps. Eve's ass will hit the roof if she found out, and finding out from another woman is always bad. So mums the word. I gotta make some moves so we will have to continue this conversation a little later."

I hung up the phone thinking that all these relationships are bull. People hopping in or falling out of love or sleeping with this person or that person. I knew none of this could have been good, but fuck it, what was I gonna do about it. Eve is always walking around here hollering 'my man is different'. What the hell ever!

I walked back to my bedroom and lay across my bed eager to call Gerald but I knew I would see him later on tonight hell I couldn't help the excitement that was taking over my body.

Hell I don't know what the hell is wrong with my ass but I knew Gerald was part of the problem or part of a beginning.

Chapter 26

Date night

What should I wear? I skimmed through my closet, picking this shirt or these jeans. Damn why was I so nervous? It's not like I haven't been to his house before. "Okay April, calm your ass down." I decided to wear a turquoise wrap dress that flared at the bottom with a V shapes neckline and topped it off with a pair of white and turquoise wedge Giuseppe's. Damn I am ready to go all in tonight. There's nothing like being with a man who really wants you. Now don't get me wrong, Gerald has womanizer written all over him, so I have to play my cards right and keep my eye on him. Hell, I am not mad at nobody. If you can play the game and win, then play, but when asked a simple question pertaining to possibly cheating on someone just answer the damn question truthfully. Look at Drew, he is about to lose his damn mind. And over what? Another woman's pussy. And I know for sure he is not admitting to cheating on Stephanie.

Seriously when that texting started between us I should have stopped it, but I didn't. We did it, now it's over with. I just hope this crazy ass fuck gets the message.

Even though me and Gerald were not seeing each other till later I knew I had to get my things in order such as the basics to sex night. Make sure Miss Kitty is waxed perfectly; facial, I want to glow under candle light; and the perfect panties and bra, as sexy as Gerald makes me feel I think I am going to wear the hipster thongs with lace and matching lace bra and of course my favorite color red.

There was a knock on my door I was almost afraid to answer; I wasn't trying to get another surprise package left on my door step. I walked to the door with ease and low and behold who the fuck did I see staring back at me through my peep hole…Gerald. Oh my goodness I got on a robe and no clothes, my nipples are getting hard just by him standing out there. Oh shit what am I gonna do? Guess I have no other choice but to let him in…here goes nothing.

I swung the door open, and was instantly hit with his gorgeous smile and pretty white teeth. "Hey Gerald come on in." I stepped to the side and let him enter my sanctuary.

"Hey, beautiful I was on my way to do some errands and looked up and saw that I was passing your neighborhood. I hope it is okay that I stopped by. I know I should have called first, but when I looked up I was already here."

I looked at Gerald as if to say who the hell you fooling. I guess I passed the ole drop by to make sure there is no one else up in my bed test. "It is perfectly fine I am really glad to see you, so what are you out doing this early in the day."

"Well, for starters got to get my car detailed and get dinner for us tonight. I want a perfect night with you so I must start things early."

I think he just won some brownie points.

"Do you wanna run around town with me? We can do this together and just spend more time together. I can wait till you get dressed, I'm in no hurry."

Now I'm blushing and shit. Yeah Gerald is a smooth talking brother and his deep voice just adds to his sex appeal. I walked right up to him and stood on my tippy toes, wrapped my arms around his neck, and planted a kiss firmly on his lips. I have been wanting to do that since he walked in here looking damn good I must say. He was dressed sexy casual, a pair of black slacks, a grey collard Polo shirt topped off with a pair of black Hugo Boss Newar Oxfords. Damn this man even knew how to look good on the weekends, and here I stand in a red satin robe and nothing else. I wondered what he was thinking. He has looked me up and down a few times and each time he has licked his lips, that's code for I wonder what you taste like.

I wanted to let him taste me right then and there but for some reason I wanted to save it for later on tonight. I wanted to feel like I was saving it for him. Yeah, yeah I know it sounds crazy since I am nowhere near a virgin, but the thought that he is wanting me in a way that goes beyond sexual is gratifying.

"I am glad you did that. I didn't want to seem too presumptuous; those lips have been calling me since I walked in. That has brightened my day babe."

Did he just call me babe? Is he serious? We have been on a couple lunch dates and a dinner at his house and I'm babe all ready. I could get use to this shit. He better sit still for a minute before he's putting his and hers bath towels in his bathroom.

"Although hanging with you is a bit tempting, I also have a few errands I need to run. So can I see you later tonight?"

His smiled faded, but then he nodded. "Yeah, that's cool. I just thought I'd ask. No worries."

160

The ladies of Delphine Publications

Walking Gerald to the door, we made small talk. The sexual tension was in the air and I had to get him out of here immediately. Once I opened the door he turned and looked at me, no words were spoken just him leaning in for another kiss this time more sensual and longer.

Gerald cleared his throat before he spoke. "I will see you later and don't keep me waiting. I cannot wait till I see you tonight."

With a wink of his eye he walked back to his car. Just watching him walk away turned me on. As he was starting to pull away I closed the door. I went into my bedroom and looked at the clock on the night stand it was 1 p.m. and it was time to get my waxing, nails, toes, and hair done. I wanted to look my best. Fifteen minutes later I heard my doorbell ring. I immediately smiled thinking that Gerald just couldn't stay away so I ran to the door. This time I had the belt a little loose, that way he could see a peek of my breasts. Making my way to the door, my nipples harden at the anticipation. I flung the door open and to my surprise it was Drew's ass!

"Lawd what the fuck are you doing here again?"

Drew pushed past me and forced his way in, demanding that I close the door quickly.

"So you're dating now? Just that quick you've found someone?"

I started fuming at the nerve of this asshole, granted he is an asshole with great dick but still an asshole. I immediately covered my almost exposed breasts.

"You don't come over here wondering who I'm seeing or who I'm dating Drew. Why the hell aren't you in your own damn house? Please don't tell me you woke up early this morning to come and harass me.

"Hell no, but I'm curious to know how one minute you're fucking me like I am all that you care about then the next you having lunch with other dudes like I don't fucking matter. What the fuck is up with that shit April?"

"I don't have to explain shit to you Drew! I am not your wife. We were just fucking. That's it, that's all and I am not gonna keep having the same damn conversation with you. But seriously though it is time for you to leave and stay away from me. This shit is almost stalking. You do know that don't you Drew?" I have a good mind to call Stephanie and tell her come get her husband once and for all. This shit has gotten out of hand.

"No you don't have to explain shit to me. This thing with you and I is pretty much done anyway, so I could care less who you are seeing now."

I knew that was bullshit.

Drew sat on the sofa and placed his head in his hands. I closed my robe even tighter, because my kit-kat was starting to act up just knowing what he can do with his dick and that mouth of his…I'm in trouble. I moved closer to him and sat down slowly on the couch next to him, since this was new news to me, I had to hear him out. Last I heard he didn't want me with Gerald and he wanted me to be his side piece.

"So now you've suddenly gotten over me? What happen to all this love mess, Drew? Now you could care less."

"I love my wife and my children April. What we did had my nose wide open and the way things were going between Steph and I, I confused my sexual emotions with love. Stephanie was a terrible wife. A certain time to do this a certain time to do that, that damn woman even had me on a sex schedule. That shit was ridiculous. And you, I mean you are gorgeous, spontaneous, and you do things that my wife used to frown on, but since that day I walked out on her, and she realized what she had, things have been different. I came by to tell you that what I did with you was so wrong. I'm sorry for even putting you in that type of situation, because I know you and Stephanie are friends." He stood. "If she ever found out about us, she'd hate us both. I hate that I went there with you. I'm sorry for stalking you and acting like a lunatic. The chemistry between us was insane and that's what had me running behind you like a puppy, but now I'm going to make things right with Steph, so I wish you well."

Drew looked down at me. I immediately thought about standing up and opening the door to let his ass out, but he looked so damn sexy. The thought of sex with him came over me and my kit-kat was now popping ready to be licked. Now it was me, I wanted the finale and then I'd let him be.

"Wait Drew please don't go. I know you're going to work things out with Stephanie, and that is a good thing, but I gotta admit I missed you." I stood and let my robe fall open for him to get a look at my hardened nipples. I knew he wouldn't be able to resist, he reached in and rubbed my protruding nipples. I tilted my head back. As always it felt so good.

"Lay back baby and let me taste you."

Now who was I to not let him taste my sweetness? I was willing to have my clit licked good one last time before I let Gerald sample my sweetness.

"Go ahead baby lick on this pussy one last time."

I laid back and Drew removed my robe to expose my full size breasts and my kit-kat was purring and ready to go. Drew began sucking on each nipple and caressing my breast tenderly. My legs fell apart slightly and with his other hand he cupped my fat kit-kat and slipped in a finger, once he curved it and gave my pussy the come here sign that was about to send me over the edge. I see he wanted to have me squirting all over the place.

"Come on Drew eat this pussy for me, it's so wet and ready for you."

Drew dove in with no problem to taste my sweet juices. Damn this shit felt so good I was thinking I should let him back in my life. Hell no just eat me so I can get off then go to your wife. All I was hearing was slurp, slurp, slurp. He spread my lips apart and pulled back the hood to my clit and that did it for me. I was counting down from ten and when I got to one I exploded all over him and my couch. My body was shaking and it had tensed up so I caught his head in between my thighs.

"Damn baby you are a champ when it comes to eating pussy. Shit I love this shit."

Drew got up and went to the bathroom to clean off his mouth and I laid there and continued to rub my kit-kat because the trembles were still in me. Patting my pussy I was damn near ready for round two but quickly thought against that since I was going to see Gerald later on.

I got up off the couch and walked to my bedroom and saw the light blinking on my phone. I grabbed my phone and saw I had a missed call from Eve. I didn't want to call anyone at this moment but I needed a distraction so Drew would get the hint that it was time for him to go. So I called Eve back hoping it wasn't nothing about her damn wedding.

"Hello."

"Hey Eve, I see I got a missed call from you. What's going on with you?"

"April I am so glad you called. Stephanie has called me crying hysterically."

I repeated what I just heard loudly so Drew could hear me. He came out of the bathroom with the look of confusion on his face.

"What the hell is wrong with her now?"

"This is serious April. I didn't want to say anything, but Stephanie thinks he's cheating and even though they are working things out, she still thinks he is messing around on her."

"I'm sorry to hear that, but what are we supposed to do about it. I am not about to get all up in married folks' business like that and I honestly think she's imagining things. Drew is too afraid of her ass to cheat." I chuckled.

"April she is our sorority sister, we have to be there for her. I am on my way over there. Do you want to meet me there or should I come and get you?"

"No, neither one! I have plans and dealing with Stephanie and her tears is something that I just don't want to do right now but I will check back and see how she doing. Sorry, I really do have other plans."

I hung up the phone and got instantly pissed off.

"Is something wrong with my wife?" Drew said as he walked closer to me searching for answers that were not written on my face.

"The only thing that is wrong with her is the fact that your ass is here and not there. She knows you're fucking around Drew?"

"Impossible."

"Dammit Drew, not impossible. She called Eve hysterically over your ass."

Drew hurried to the front door like I didn't say two words to him. He opened my door and looked at me. "Good luck with Gerald, this is the last time you will ever see me. I love Stephanie. Fucking around with you was low and I hope I can fix things with Stephanie."

His eyes glossed and at that moment, I could see that he really loved that controlling chick. He hurried out and I said, "Good luck with that," before heading to my room to call Gerald.

Chapter 27

Eve

It was a beautiful Monday morning with only five days left until Jared and I are officially married. Everything was on point from the food, venue, décor, invitations, and even the cake. Jared finally came with me to see the progress of our beautiful five tier cake accented with our favorite colors; pink and blue.

I was glad that my sorority sisters finally got their dresses despite the drama that came with it. How we all managed to stay friends stilled baffled me. I know one thing for sure I will have to keep Jared away from Keli. Even though I do believe him about giving her a ride home because she was wasted and the two of them telling me nothing happen, I still had that ugly little itch that I can't seem to scratch because my thing is why didn't he go home instead of me finding his car in her driveway the next morning.

I am a Christian so I just have to faith in Jared because he is my future husband and I don't want to have a marriage that's not based on trust, but at the same time I'm not stupid either. Now that my wedding was on point, I needed my sisters to be seriously on point and if that means strapping their behinds in a chair and in a room, then that's just what I will have to do. There is no way I am going to let them ruin my special day.

I had to set up the friend's night out that Stephanie suggested. I invited Steph, April and Heaven. I also invited Delilah behind Steph's back so they could squash all this silly nonsense that has gotten them acting like preschoolers all because of this Drew fellow. I was honestly nervous about having them in the same room, but this is something that must be done. I had asked Heaven not to tell Stephanie or Delilah that either one of them was coming.

I had everyone to meet at my house around 8pm. Heaven was the first to arrive. Heaven and I took our seats in the living room. I had some Pepsi, bottled water, and a large cheese and cracker platter on the coffee table in front of us. I knew better than to serve alcohol because from all of our previous girl's night outs that alcohol and my sisters do not mix well.

Heaven was dressed fabulously in her cream camisole, fitted jeans, and black blazer. I went for more of a light blue shirt, beige slacks, and rounded it off with a pair of beige heels.

"Did you tell Stephanie that Delilah was coming?" Heaven asked as she picked up a cheese cracker off the platter.

"I sure didn't. If I did neither one of them would have come. I hope you didn't tell Delilah that Stephanie was coming?" I took a swallow from the Pepsi can that I just opened.

"No, of course not! I just hope you know what you are doing," she shot back.

We both laughed, but on the serious note I wanted Stephanie and Delilah to spend some time together and rekindle that sister's love. I also took this opportunity to address the situation between her and Keli.

"Speaking on the topic of Stephanie and Delilah, how about you and Keli do a sit down, too?"

"Well, I thought I could trust her because we're supposed to be sisters but to tell you the truth I wanted to slap that bitch and Quinton's ass too."

"I don't understand why you all are letting a man come between you guys' relationship. I know what Keli is doing is wrong, but at the same time, Quinton is really playing both of you. I just hope and pray that for this one day my special day that everyone acts like decent human beings. I need you and Keli there, so please can you do this favor for me." I beg her like I was child getting ready to get discipline from my parents.

"I'll do it for you, but if Keli says one word to me I'ma beat the ratchetness out of her ass."

"Don't worry I'll talk to her, too." I was finally able to breathe easily.

"So tell me why a great Christian woman like yourself wants to marry Jared?" She asked with a chuckle. "We all know Jared probably ain't set one foot inside anybody's church."

"Well, I was raised in a two parent Christians home surrounded by love and moral values."

"Really!" Heaven laughed. "I'm not laughing at you because I respect you very much, it's Jared. I don't think he was brought up in the church."

"He is still a decent and loving man, Heaven." I shot her a smile.

"I'm sure he is," she grinned.

"Like I was saying; my father was pastor at our church back home in Detroit. He was our family's third generation to take over as Pastor when my grandfather passed away."

Heaven reached over and placed her hands over mine. "I am so sorry about your grandfather. I know he is smiling down right on you."

I patted her hands. "It's okay, thanks. My mother was also brought up in the faith and she would constantly remind me not to spread my legs to any man unless he was my husband and I strongly believe that and hold true to family values."

"Yes, I see and you're a good one because I know I would go crazy." Heaven chuckled. "Where are they?"

"They should be here soon, unless they both pulled up together and got into a fight and got hauled off to jail." I said.

"I really do hope you know what you are doing?"

"Of course," I walked over to the closet by the front door to get my trusted side kick which was my bible. "I got this on standby." I returned to the living room, laughing, but I was dead serious.

"Damn! Let's just hope it don't go that far." Heaven chuckle.

Before I could respond, I heard the doorbell. "Well, our first guest is here." I took a deep breath and walked over to the front door.

"Are you sure you know what you are doing?" Heaven asked.

Without answering her, I open the door to see Stephanie standing there looking fabulous as usually. I gave her a cheek to cheek kiss before moving to the side to let her in. "I am so glad you could make it. I wasn't sure if you was going to show up," I said as I try to tune out Heaven's chuckling.

"I wouldn't miss spending time with my friends, and I am so glad you took me up on my offer about having a girl's night out with just us four," Stephanie said as she made her made to sofa.

"Well April isn't coming. She didn't know we'd have another girl's night out since the fiasco at Keli's, so she had plans."

"Hey, Steph. I love that purse you are rocking." Heaven took another cheese cracker. "You are just in time to have a light snack and don't overlook the non-alcoholic drinks.

I took my seat next to Stephanie. "The point is and all that matters is that we are together."

Stephanie burst out laughing. "I didn't mean to laugh at you, Eve, I know you don't drink, but we all shouldn't have to suffer. Girl, where is the wine and the rest of drinks? You know…something with alcohol."

"You can't be serious! When alcohol gets involved it becomes a living nightmare and I can't stand it."

"Fine then I'm just glad we could have this chance to talk about all the drama that went on the last time we were at Keli's. I hope that you're not going to let Keli be in your wedding after what happen between her and Jared." Stephanie rolled her eyes like she was irritated.

I narrowed my eyes at her because she was way out of line. "First of all, didn't nothing happen between them and you are taking things way too far. Jared told me what really happened."

Heaven clenched her teeth. "So you believe Jared and Keli? Keli is nothing but a home wrecker and a liar. If she's going to be in your wedding then you can count me out too."

Stephanie chimed in. "That's right. If that ratchet ass Keli and Delilah are still going to be in the wedding then you can count me out too!"

"Just wait a minute! Nobody is pulling out of nothing. It doesn't have to be this way and you guys are going too far."

"No we have not. We haven't gone far enough!" Stephanie said, turning up her nose. "And another thing…I am getting sick and tired of all the drama every time we have a meet up."

"What?" I retorted.

Heaven smack her lips. "Stephanie is right. I feel the same way. It's just too much and it's becoming a hot mess."

I inhale deeply, let out an exasperated sigh, and shake my head. "I truly can understand why you two don't want to do girl's night out anymore because I was feeling the same way, but didn't know how to say it."

"Really!" Heaven shrieks.

"Yeah, I see it was getting to you two as well." Stephanie said bitterly, "I am too much of a woman to be around back stabbing ho's."

I shook my head in disbelief. "You are not understanding why I got you all here. I didn't invite you over here so we could bash our sisters." I took another deep breath. "I wanted you two to come over because I want all my sorority sisters in my wedding. I have planned a rehearsal dinner in two days and I need all of my sisters there and not to mention on your best behavior.

"I don't know, but I will not tolerate bullshit from Keli or Quinton," Heaven spat.

"Exactly! I'll just bring some gym shoes just in case a bitch gets out of line," Stephanie waves her hand.

Before I could say another word, I heard a knock at the door. I purposely glared into Stephanie's eyes. "Please behave."

Stephanie looked confused. She shot an eye at Heaven who hunched her shoulder like she didn't know what was going on.

Then she glared at me. "Why are you looking at me like that and why do I have to behave?"

I prayed silently before I open the door because I knew it's was going to involved to some kind of altercation.

"Hey, Delilah, come in." I said giving her a cheek to cheek kiss.

"Hey, Eve!" Delilah smiled. "What you got to eat because I am starving."

"I got some pop and some light snacks in the living room."

The second Delilah walked into the living room everything went into high gear.

"Oh hell nah! What hell is she doing here?" Delilah yelled.

I held Delilah by her arms. "You will sit next to Heaven on the opposite side of coffee table because I don't need anyone throwing blows at each other."

"I don't need no drama in my life right now." Stephanie stood as she was getting ready to leave.

"No, I want you to sit down and let's talk this out!" I waited till Delilah sat down before I made my way over to Stephanie. "No need for you two to act like this." I pulled her by the arm to sit as I sat down.

"Just hear her out." Heaven tried to reason with them both.

"You didn't tell me she was going to be here Eve." Stephanie rolled her eyes at Delilah before looking at me.

"I know she didn't just roll her eyes at me!" Delilah retorted while Heaven patted her on her arm to notation her to hush up.

"I looked directly at Stephanie. "If I would have told you then you probably wouldn't have come," I replied.

"You're damn right." Stephanie replied back.

"Listen ladies, I really want you two to stop this foolishness because I know it stems from Drew. This man got you all acting unladylike." I shook my head.

"We know you have your wedding coming up and I'm giving everyone a chance and be there just for you," Delilah said.

"Oh girl puh'lease." Stephanie rolled her eyes. "Your ass is so damn fake and phony."

"You got a lot of nerve calling somebody phony with your stuck up ass. I see why Drew wants to leave you," Delilah yelled.

"What?" Stephanie said, shocked. "Drew ain't going nowhere honey so get your facts straight."

"Oh, really! Because it's no secret that I can't stand your ass or the fact that Drew can't either!" Delilah spat.

"I don't have time for this." Stephanie stood up again with her purse wrapped around her hands.

"Stop it!" I yelled. I pointed at the sofa like I was the parent and she was the child. "Sit down now!" Then I gave Delilah a stern look. "You sit there and shut up and listen." I was getting agitated with the both of them.

"Well, now we're getting somewhere," Heaven said. "Guys, you see you are upsetting Eve. Can we all at least be polite during the rehearsal dinner and most importantly, the wedding? I even promise to act civil myself. Just remember that we are doing this for Eve."

"Fine!" Delilah rolled her eyes and looked at Stephanie.

"I am only doing this for Eve and on that note I'm out of here." Stephanie grabbed her purse and walked out the door.

"I just want to say that I am going to be the bigger person and say that I am sorry for the way I have acted in your home Eve." Delilah stood up followed by me and Heaven. "I really would like to be in your wedding, but I'll say this," she walked to the door, then turned around and looked me in the eye. "You need to watch her because this isn't the last time that heifer is going to act like she lost her damn mind."

"I say we all should call it a truce and be there for our girl Eve," Heaven said as she walks to the door with me right behind her.

"That is all that I asked you all to do. Behave and be there for me." I took a deep breath to calm myself down.

"You will be a whole lot calmer if you didn't invite Stephanie." Delilah twisted her lips. "I'll see you later."

I just shook my head as I closed the door, ending a day of pure exhaustion. I couldn't say that I was overjoyed with the outcome, but at least it's a start. I still needed to convince Keli not to back out of the wedding. Truth be told, I was really at my wits end with my sorority sisters and once this wedding is finally over with maybe then I will have my sanity back.

Chapter 28

THE NEXT DAY

I woke up early feeling more drained and stressed than usual. I am supposed to feel happy and excited about getting married, but I'm not. I have four days left before I am to be a new bride and the future Mrs. Jared Lee Mosley. Instead, I just keep getting these horrible images of my dinner rehearsal party turning into a disaster and is something that I cannot face. This might just be the worst dinner party and wedding event ever. My nerves were shot, I could feel it moving to the pit of stomach and it was making me very sick.

I heard my phone rang, picked it up hoping it was Jared on the other end. To my surprise, it was my wedding planner and fellow church member, Brenda.

"Hey, Brenda." I tried to sound energetic, but couldn't.

"I'm glad you are up because we need to talk and I am five minutes away."

"How you know I didn't have other plans this early in the morning?"

"The only plans you should have this morning is making sure everyone is on time for this wedding, and I like my coffee with two cream and two sugars. Gotta go," Brenda said before she hung up.

"Seriously!" I pulled back the sheets, put on my pink house shoes, and headed to the kitchen to make me some coffee in my comfortable pink and yellow plaid pajama pants and a pink shirt.

I make some pancakes, eggs and cheese, and oatmeal. Fifteen minutes later, I heard the doorbell. "I'm coming." I took a few slow steps to the front door.

"Good morning," Brenda said in her cheery tone.

I closed the door behind her and slowly walked back to the kitchen with her on my heels being overjoyed and happy.

"I don't know what's so good about it because if you have friends like mine you wouldn't be saying that."

"Oh, couldn't be that bad." She tried to sound sincere.

Once Brenda sat down, I fix her a plate and sat her cup of coffee in front of her. I grabbed my plate and coffee and sat opposite of her. I would usually dive into my food, but when things are going crazy I tend to just pick at it.

I wonder how she would feel if I told her that I don't want to do this dinner rehearsal or have a wedding. What if Jared and I just elope? How would I break the news to her? "Yes, really. I don't know what to do?" I sipped my coffee.

"How many times did I tell you that God got this under control? You just have to pray about it and just let God handle it. I'm pretty sure your friends know this means the world to you." Brenda picked up her fork and ate her pancakes. "If they don't then shame on them."

I gave a half smile to calm my nerves. "I hope they do. I keep drilling it in their mind that my wedding day has to be perfect."

"I mean you really don't have to invite them."

"I can't do that! Then I will feel guilty."

"Guilty! Guilty about what? You should be overjoyed and dancing, instead you're up here in your night clothes and picking at your food."

"I know and I am really thinking seriously about having a wedding." I struggled to collect my thoughts. "I don't know if I can go through with this wedding. I mean maybe Jared and I should elope, but I want to have a wedding so bad. I have my whole family coming as well as Jared's."

"Eve, honey, you will be surprised at how God can work miracles. Sure they are fighting and arguing now, but by time you walk down that aisle they will be a whole new person. Trust and believe in him because I have seen it happen plenty of times."

"I don't know, Brenda, I mean these women has cause me so much pain, grief, and havoc all rolled up in one." I took a sip of my coffee. "It's like they are wrapped up in their own world with these unfaithful men."

Brenda reached her hand over my mine and cupped them. "That's because they don't have the same spiritual upbringing that you have, but luckily they have you as a listening ear and as a confidant. All of you are very successful, strong black women and I think you all can get along once everyone sits down and talks it out."

"Truthfully, we did. I had a sit down with Heaven, Steph, and Delilah. I just need to have a sit down with Keli next. Also, I made up my mind and I really don't want to do another girl's night out either."

"Really!" Brenda was completely shock.

"I wasn't the only one thinking about calling it off. I'm just tired of all the drama every time we meet up together."

"Then listen to your heart, Eve. If you all feel like your relationship has outgrown itself then maybe you all need to move on."

"All I want to do is be with Jared forever and live my life with my husband. I think it would be good for Jared to keep his distance as well."

"Well before we get to that part I have made the arrangements for dinner rehearsal in two days so just make sure everyone is there and most importantly on time." Brenda took a sip of her coffee. "Have you spoken to Jared?"

"No, not yet. I'll give him a call before I head out."

"Head out! Head out where?" Brenda said, shocked.

"Yes, out. Is there a problem?"

"No, I just hope you and Jared are going to see the venue to make sure everything is good to go."

"I know I can trust you with whatever you have done," I reassured her.

"So, where are you heading out to?"

"I am heading over to Keli's house to convince her not to back out of the wedding, so wish me luck." I sprang from my seat. "Now if you don't mind I have to get ready."

Brenda finished her last bit of breakfast. "All I got to say is pray about it and let God do the rest. Just don't forget to call Jared because I want to see the both of you guys at the venue before everyone else arrives."

"Yes, I will do that." I walked Brenda to the front door. "You're right. I have to faith and believe that God will not let me down," I finally said before I closed the door.

179

I could do better than that. I would drive by Jared's place before heading over Keli's. I went back into the kitchen, grabbed my coffee, and headed to bedroom. I looked through my closet to find something that was comfortable to wear. I searched through a few items and decided on wearing a cute purple and white knee-length dress and white shoes that were perfect for the summer. I turned on the clock radio that was on my nightstand. I want to listen to some much needed gospel and I was just in time to hear Yolanda Adams blaring through the speakers. That woman has been truly blessed with a wonderful voice. I went into my bathroom with the music playing loud as I jumped into the shower. Once I was done, I got dressed, finished off my coffee, and I was on way to Jared's.

It took me thirty-two minuets to get to Jared's street. I must admit that my lack of interest in Jared was for good reasons. He wasn't making much money, even though I don't consider myself a gold digger. But a man has to be able to provide for his family and of course if a man wants to date me, he has to have the finances to do so. He wasn't into church, even though it was a stumbling block for me, but spending more time with him made it easy to look over that.

Here I am driving over to his house, remembering something my parents told me as I was growing up. 'A man without faith is a man without morals and God's spiritual guidance.' I was in love and I was excited to have a husband that was all about love, honor, and being faithful. He was far from Drew and Quinton. Yes, Jared was cut from another piece of cloth that was for sure.

When I got near his house, I couldn't help but notice that his car wasn't park out front or in his driveway. I just shrug it off, thinking maybe he has it in the shop. I know he told me he wanted to get it painted, so that's probably where it is. I parked my car, got out, and rang his door bell. No answer. This time I pound on the door.

"Jared, wake up!" I yelled.

I rang and pounded on his door a few more times before I retrieved my cell phone out of my purse and dialed his number.

The phone continued to ring and then finally Jared answered. "Hello."

"Hey, honey. Hope I didn't wake you? It sounds like you're sleeping."

"Maybe because I'm tired with the wedding coming up. How are you doing this morning?"

"I'm doing fine, confused and annoyed as usual," I stressed. "I was just calling to check on you."

"I'm doing good. What happened now?"

I noticed the curtain was open so I looked through the front window hoping to see a glimpse of Jared. I know he's here because he was sounding like I just woke him from a deep sleep.

"The problem is you're not here when I need you," I said pissed. "The whole situation with Stephanie, Delilah, and now Keli wanting to pull out of the wedding. I need to talk to you." I kept pounding on the door.

"What's that noise?" Jared asked.

"It's me!" I snapped. I was puzzled as to why he wasn't coming to the door. "Where are you? Are you still in bed or something? Because I am standing outside your front door."

"You're where? Why didn't you called first?" He sounded like he was wide awake then and shocked.

"Excuse me! I am your future wife and I shouldn't have to call when I want to come by! Seriously, Jared, what kind of question is that?"

"Look, calling would give me a heads up, so I can be home, dressed, or just ready to have you over."

"Whatever Jared, where are you at anyway? Because if I remember correctly you are on vacation from work."

"Well, I uh…uh had car problems so I had to get up early and take it to the shop. Why don't we meet up later and have lunch? I should be out of here soon, but I can't guarantee when they're going be finished with car."

I let out a sigh of relief that he was at the shop. I should have known better than let my imagination get the best of me. "I would love that."

"I just want to make sure everything goes perfect for the wedding and making sure that my ride is running is a must."

"Believe me I completely understand, I'm just happy to hear that you're at the shop. Look, I don't want to keep you, but I'm about to head over to Keli's so I can talk to her about this wedding."

"No, wait!" I could hear the skepticism in his voice. "I know you have a lot on your mind and this wedding is causing you a lot of stress. Baby, if you want me to talk to Keli I wouldn't mind. I don't want you to worry any more than you have to. I'll do my part to make sure our day, especially your day, is perfect."

"Thanks, Jared. I can't believe you would do that for me." I felt a little relieved because he was willing to talk to Keli on my behalf. Now I was able to focus on more important things like the upcoming rehearsal dinner and the wedding.

"I love you Eve and I live to make you happy. I just want you to know that." I could hear the sigh of relief in his voice. "So what time do you want to meet up for lunch?"

"I have to go in to work today so I'm going to have to cancel. Can we meet for dinner at my house?" I said as I walked off his front porch.

"Sure, that would be great. I will be there around five. Love you."

"I love you, too. Look, I gotta go, but I will see you this evening." I ended my call, got in my car, and pulled off.

Chapter 29

Enough is enough. I was too smart, too beautiful, and too good to be played by Drew. He didn't know me apparently and he didn't know that I'd be the one to check behind his ass, yes check. I couldn't track his purchases, since he decided to withdraw cash, but the cell phones were in both of our names and it was time for me to take a look at his call history.

Something I'd never do on an ordinary basis, but I needed to know. Since I was dedicated to working my marriage out I needed the doubts of his fidelity to be gone. I had loosened up a bit. I stopped being so controlling. Well, I eased up as much as I could comfortably do, because change never came easy. Sex was no longer a scheduled thing, I was now fucking him all over the house and we did it whenever he wanted to do it. I hated that I felt that he was still creeping.

Examining the bill, I was stunned to see a number that was familiar to me. A number that I knew well. I wondered why it was on Drew's outgoing and incoming list more often than I was comfortable with.

It couldn't be. "Not her, not her," I said as I looked at some of the back to back calls and the times he had called her or when she called him. Hours when a married man shouldn't be dialing another woman's number. My heart stopped, my stomach churned, my temples flared, and my palms began to sweat. "No, no, please no, not April. Not my sister," I winced. My heart was broken. Betrayal, confusion, disappointment, hurt, you name it hit me all at once.

I hit print and then grabbed a highlighter. I combed the bill like I was a detective working on a murder case. I wanted to highlight every call, every minute, and every second that my sorority sister and my husband shared a conversation or even when their calls went unanswered.

The pages glowed with the color of neon pink and again I found myself crying over Drew. I loved that man with everything. Controlling, yes I was. Demanding, hey, yes that was me, but I was a faithful wife. I was a committed wife and a good friend. April and I had never had beef. Yes a sisterly quarrel every now and again, but to fuck my husband, how could she? How could she? How could she? I wondered as I dialed Eve.

"He's cheating, he's still cheating Eve," I cried into the phone as soon as she answered.

"Stephanie, hold on darling. Calm down. We've talked about this. You forgave him."

"I did, but he is still creeping around Eve, I know it. I know it," I cried. I was too ashamed to tell her that he had the nerve to stoop so low to sleep with April.

"You got to be mistaken Steph. I'm sure he is no longer carrying on the affair. I can guarantee that your marriage is going to be fine."

"No it's not. Drew has crossed the line Eve. I have to put his ass out. He has no respect for me. No respect for this marriage. He has done the unthinkable Eve and I can't allow him to make a fool out of me." I wanted to tell her that he had been fucking

April, but how true was that. The only proof I had was her number painted all over his phone records.

"Stephanie, be rational honey. Drew loves you. You two had problems. You admitted it and you said you would forgive him. You said you wanted to work it out."

"I can't, I can't, I can't, not after this," I said sobbing like a big baby. This was a low for Drew and I knew I'd punch him in the fucking face when I saw him.

"Sit tight Stephanie, I'm coming," she said and hung up.

I tried to wipe my face, but the tears were relentless. I couldn't wipe them away fast enough from my drenched face. I rushed over to the bar and poured me a stiff one and then another one and then another. I went up to my bedroom and snatched open his walk in. I looked around the neatly arranged organized space and turned into a mad woman.

I snatched suits, ties, shirts, and shoes, from their resting places, rushed out to the hall, and threw them over the banister and they all hit the foyer floor. We had a grand staircase that spiraled and a beautiful crystal chandelier hanging over the grand entrance, but the space was now decorated with Drew's clothes and personal items.

I was going back and forth and I didn't stop until every hanger, drawer and shelf was empty. He had to go. He had to get the fuck out of my house. I didn't deserve a two-timing liar that wanted to fuck family. Yes, family. My sorority sisters were like my family and this was a low blow; a gut puncher and I was furious. The doorbell chimed. I didn't want to go down, but I knew it was Eve.

I opened the door and when she walked in she saw all of Drew's things covering the foyer floor. "Steph baby, what did you do?"

"He has to go Eve. He is no longer welcome in this house," I said.

"Stephanie, you can't just tossed your husband out like garbage, you have to talk to him, ask him Stephanie."

"Fuck that Eve. I'm not like you. You walk on eggshells around Jared, like that motherfucker's shit don't stink. I've never said anything because I've never wanted to hurt your feelings, but you're marrying the wrong guy. I can see right through his transparent ass. He's a dog Eve. Men like Jared don't go without hitting something. But since you walk around in your own little Christian world with blinders, as if you don't see what's really going on, I stay out of it."

"All the times your calls go unanswered Eve, when you spend hours not hearing from his ass, or when he can't show up to simply pick out china for your wedding, it's his wedding too! Come on Eve, open your eyes," I said.

I never liked Jared, but I've never voiced it or said a word to Eve, because she was truly my best friend of them all. I mean Heaven and I were super tight too, but Heaven and I didn't share what Eve and I did.

"Stephanie, I came here to console you, not to be attacked. Just because Drew is out of order, don't go speaking things about Jared. You don't know him Stephanie. You've never even tried to get to know him. So don't you stand here and speak ill about him." Eve's eyes glossed as if she knew that I was right, but she was too blinded by so called love to be honest with herself, so I felt bad.

"You're right and I'm sorry. I'm just so angry. Drew is the love of my life Eve. I pardoned his infidelity because I knew I was a tyrant. After we reconciled, I thought he'd end it, but he's out late, keeps blaming it on caseloads and then tonight…" I paused. I didn't want to tell her about April. "Tonight I'm home alone again. I took the kids to my parents to have some time, but I get his voicemail. I'm not going to sit back and watch him fuck over me. He's got the wrong one Eve. He has to go."

"Stephanie you're jumping to conclusions. Drew loves you and everyone knows that. He has been madly in love with you since college. Even the B in you," she said. I laughed. She acted as God would just strike her down if she dared to say one bad word.

"It's not the same," I whimpered. "We've drifted apart." She held me. A few moments later Drew walked in from the kitchen. We both looked up at him. He saw my face, drenched in tears.

"Steph, baby, what's wrong," he rushed over.

"Eve please go so I can talk to my husband."

"Are you sure Stephanie? Maybe you should come with me and sleep on this and talk tomorrow."

"No, it's time to handle this." I stood. "I'll walk you out." I could see the terror in Drew's eyes. His ass was guilty and I knew it.

After hugging Eve and guaranteeing her that my situation with Drew would not stop me from being a part of her wedding she left.

Back inside I could see fear all over Drew's face and the look of sadness in his eyes.

"Are you going to tell me the truth or do I have to pry it out of you?" I asked standing in the entryway of our living room with my hands on my hips. My chest rose and fell at a steady rhythm as I coached myself to remain calm.

"I'm sorry Stephanie. We were at a bad place and I...I...I needed what you weren't willing to offer at the time...but since we've reconciled, I swear that I've been on the straight and narrow."

That came out of his mouth so smooth and so quick, for the first time I couldn't detect if it was rehearsed or the truth.

"I've known about your indiscretions for a long time Drew. The cash withdrawals, the 'I'm working late', the change in your step when you walked, or how you'd leave up out of here tense and stressed and come home late, relaxed and at ease.

"I knew that part of it was me, that I knew, and the night when you walked out and didn't come home for two days, I blamed myself. I told myself that I had to now be the one to change, so you could be happy too and I was willing to do whatever to win back your heart," I said softly. My eyes were flooded with water and my vision had become cloudy, so I blinked for my tears to fall.

He stood and walked in my direction. "I never stopped loving you Steph. I still love you baby and I want this marriage. I want to be here with you and our girls. I was foolish."

"You damn right you were and I would have given you the chance to get yourself together Drew, for us to try to work out our differences so we both can be happy in this relationship. But now? No, I can't."

"No, baby, don't say that," he said coming over to me.

189

"Drew don't you dare touch me."

"I messed up baby. I fucked up big time, but please don't do this. I've loved you since the day I met you Stephanie. Things just got so routine in this house. You scheduled our love making like this was your marriage and not our marriage. I put up with it, I begged you to change Stephanie and instead of you hearing me, you treated me like I was your son and not your husband. I put up with it because I loved you, and I still do, don't do this. I'll do whatever you say, we can go back to the way you want it, but please Stephanie," he cried.

I wanted to say okay but that wouldn't work. Continuing to treat him like I did before he walked out would only make him miserable and then he'd step out on me again. I was willing to relax a little, have more fun, be more spontaneous and just step out of my routine, for him. Until I figured out that he had been with April. That shit changed everything.

"Drew you can stand here and apologize and explain, but nothing is going to convince me to be with you after what you've done. My sister Drew, you fuck April and expect me to stay," I shot at him.

His mouth opened, his eyes bulged. His total expression was my confirmation that it was true.

"I...I...I," he stuttered. "Did April tell you?" He inquired.

"No, I figured it out on my own and now that I know, get the fuck out!"

"Steph, I'm so, so sorry," he said dropping to his knees.

I wanted to kick him. "Don't Drew, just go."

"No, I'm not going anywhere."

I stopped in my tracks. "Excuse me."

190

"I love you and I want to come clean with everything right now at this moment," he said. He stood and approached me. "And then I want you to forgive me and I want us to work on our marriage. I love you Stephanie and we are here right now because of us, not because of what you've done or what I've done. It's what we've done to each other and I will fight for you and this marriage. I don't give a shit what it takes."

I looked at him and wanted to laugh in his face. I admired his valiant effort because my heart was with Drew and for Drew, but the affair with April was too much.

"Drew I don't know what our future will be like, but right now, I don't want to be with you. The affair was one thing because I figured it was another lawyer, or a past client, or some trick you may have met that whispers the sweet nothings I never whispered in your ear, but April. That bitch has looked me in my face, been in this house and pretended to be a friend to me. You and I have to talk because of our girls, but that bitch, when I see her I may stomp a hole in her chest."

"I know we were foolish Stephanie and it started out—" he tried to say.

"No!" I held up my hands. "Details and how and when will only make it worse Andrew! Now please go. All of your things are in the foyer. I know you can't get them all now, but get what you need and be back tomorrow to get the rest. I'll pick up the girls from Mom's after work tomorrow and whatever's left in this house will burn in the fire pit out back."

"Stephanie," he tried to reason.

"I'm dead serious Drew."

"There's more."

"What?" My eyes darted at him. "More? What do you mean more?"

"Can we sit?"

"Hell no. Is she pregnant? Did that ho get pregnant?"

"No, no, no, she's not pregnant babe."

"Then what, huh? What else?"

"I spent one night with Delilah."

My heart stopped. My legs went wobbly, not only one, but two. My mouth opened, but nothing came out.

"Somehow she found out about April and I and she said she'd tell you if I didn't—," he was trying to say more but I slap the shit out of him.

"Get out!" I roared. "Get your stupid ass out of my house!" I said swinging wildly. I could have killed Drew in that moment. "Go, go, go, get out," I pushed him towards the door. He tried to restrain me but I was enraged.

"Baby calm down," he pleaded finally grabbing a firm hold of me. I struggled to break free but he held on to me so tight that it was useless. I became exhausted trying to break free. I just began to sob in his arms. It felt like daggers doing a drum roll in my heart. This pain that Drew put on me was unforgivable.

I knew I wanted him out of my house but now I was going to call a lawyer.

"Shhh baby. I'm sorry," he cried with me with his face in my neck. Even though he had done the ultimate, I knew it had hurt him too, but I didn't give a fuck.

After what seemed like forever, he loosened his grip and slowly released me. I didn't look back at his trifling ass I just went to the kitchen. I poured me a double shot of tequila and went over to my family room and took a seat.

I heard Drew come into the kitchen and go for the tequila too. Why was that fool still in my house?

"Steph—," he started, but I raised my hand and shook my head. My back was to him, but I heard him down his drink and place the glass on the counter. With no more words he left.

Chapter 30

I rolled out of bed and went to the bathroom. When I stood to wash my hands I didn't recognize myself in the mirror. My natural mane looked dry and my eyes were swollen like I had been in a fight.

I went for my phone, called my office, and took the day off. Something I never had done my entire career. Yes, I have had days off, but they were usually scheduled vacation time off, planned appointments for the girls, or doctor's appointments for me, but never had I ever called in.

I went to check my text messages. I had over thirty text messages from Drew, but I didn't bother to read them. I crawled back into my bed, pulled the covers over my head, and cried until I fell back to sleep. A couple of hours later I was awakened by Eve's ringtone, "Take Me to the King" by Tamela Mann. I had all of my girlfriends programmed with a unique ringtone, so I could identify who was calling when my phone wasn't within reach.

Groggy I answered, "Hello."

"Hey Steph, how are you? Did you and Drew talk it out?"

"No Eve we didn't and right now isn't a good time for me."

"You sound terrible Steph. Is there something I can do?"

"Yes, you can as a matter of fact, you can put your Jesus shoes on the shelf and roll with me to whip April and Delilah's asses."

"What? What for? Why?"

"Both of those trifling ho's have been with my husband."

"Nooooo, noooo, Stephanie, you have to be mistaken. I can't believe that."

"Well believe it Holy Spirit," I called her. I only called her that when she act as if she couldn't see beyond her holy eyes. "I'm telling you the truth. Drew has been messing around with April and Delilah decided she wants in. She threatens to tell me if Drew didn't oblige her in the bedroom. When I see them, Eve, I'm going to slap the piss out of them both. I'm done with them. There is no forgiving either of them and Drew, well he is lucky that I love living in the free world, because I would have killed him last night."

"Oh my God, this is bad. Oh Stephanie I'm so sorry. What would possess April to do something so low? I can see Delilah, she's wanted Drew since college, but April."

"Well you can stay friends with those evil bitches if you'd like, but I'm done and I don't think I can be a part of your wedding."

"Stephanie please don't say that. Please. This day means so much to me and I want you to be by my side. The only reason I didn't make you my matron of honor, is because I didn't want any conflicts. You can't bail on me Stephanie, please reconsider."

"I don't know Eve. I don't think I can stand to be in the same room with either of them."

"I know Stephanie, but you of all people can't bail on me. I need you there Stephanie. I need you. You are the only one of my sisters that I have admired for having a sound relationship. I know things are grim right now with your marriage, but I used to say 'I want what Stephanie and Drew have'. Drew messed up. I know he did, but love conquers all Stephanie. Don't let this be the end, you can forgive him and work it out."

"Fuck love Eve. Yes I've been controlling, demanding, hard to please, or even harder to live with, but I've never cheated on Drew. Never once entertained that thought and he does this to me," I said now crying. "Just think of how you felt when you thought Jared slept with Keli."

"Well Keli's a ho," Eve spat.

"And April isn't? And Delilah, I want to whip her ass even more, because she finally found a way to have my husband. I'm sorry Eve, I can't…I won't be a part of your wedding. Trust you don't want me there," I cried in the phone.

"Please Stephanie, please reconsider. After the ceremony you can leave, but can you please put all of this aside for me. I'm begging you."

"I'll let you know," I said and ended the call. I wanted to be there for Eve, but it was going to be close to impossible to put my issues on the side lines. I had a mind to get dress and pay both of them bitches a visit. Yes, that's what I'll do."

I got up threw on a pair of sweats, a long sleeved V-neck cotton shirt, and my tennis shoes. I knew I was going to open up a can on them both and I was ready to go as many rounds as it took.

I raced down the stairs, grabbed my purse and keys and as soon as I opened the door, I almost ran into Drew. I wondered why my husband decided to come back so soon and I asked myself why did he look extra fine. Damn Drew, this is too soon, I definitely didn't need to see you. I thought as I stepped aside and allowed him to come in.

Chapter 31

I sat there in a daze, wondering how I allowed Eve and Drew to convince me to wait until after the wedding to deal with April and Delilah. Eve swore she understood, but begged me to just hold my peace until she and Jared tied the knot.

She had a point that if I did confront them and fight them and things got crazy, not only would I back out, April and Delilah would also, and since Keli had already resigned, no one, but Heaven would be in her wedding. I wanted to say tough, but she begged me. Not long after I let Drew in, she showed up ringing the hell out of my doorbell. She and Drew both talked me into this bullshit and now I was sitting next to Drew with his arm over my shoulder like we had no issues.

Only Eve knew that about April and Delilah. I knew I'd tell Heaven right after the wedding. I was quiet for the first time and didn't have much to say, because I knew I'd explode if one of them bitches said the wrong thing to me. My green handbag rested across my lap. I gripped it as April spoke giving the bride and groom well wishes. I wanted to say, 'shut the fuck up. You know nothing about love, honor, and respect. How dare you let those words part your lips,' but I gritted my teeth and held on to my words.

Drew rubbed my arms to comfort me but I gave him a look and he stopped. Bad enough I was sitting next to him playing nice for Eve's sake. I didn't need him pretending to care.

Surprised when Keli walked in, we all watched her as she went over and gave Eve a hug. She whispered something in her ear and Eve smiled and gestured her to take a seat. All eyes on her, she said. "Listen, I didn't come to make waves and even though I won't be in the wedding, Eve is my sister, so I'm here. This has nothing to do with what's going on with us, so for Eve, we will chill on that." She sat and Eve's face was glowing. I was so happy that she was happy to have us all there, but she knew our shit wasn't tight.

The mic went around the room with people saying things about Eve and Jared. Folks giving speeches about love, marriage, and forgiving and it was making me angrier. My damn marriage was in the toilet and my husband kept giving me a squeeze and rubbing my arms like we were all good. By the time Delilah stood to say her well wishes I wanted to throw up. Another ho ass liar giving words of honor to marriage who cared less about mine.

"Really," I mumbled. Drew tapped me.

"Baby, you promised," he reminded me.

"I know what I said Drew," I said between clenched teeth.

"Okay," he whispered.

I sat and continued to listen to that bitch speak, wanting to cut her off, but I didn't. Finally the mic hit my hand and I stood. I turned to Eve. "Eve, my sister, my best friend, congratulations. I promised you I would be good for this occasion and I will keep that promise because I know how important this is to you and that

199

look of happiness on your face says that I'm doing the right thing." I sighed and looked around.

"Since I'm the only married person in our circle, I will be honest with you and say it has ups and downs and there will be days you may want to throw in the towel, but…" I paused and blinked back my tears. "But if you truly love him, it's okay to forgive him." Those words were true, because I had decided to forgive Drew, but that didn't mean I was going to be with him.

"Jared, whatever you do always think of Eve before you do it. Just imagine how she'd feel or the look on her face if she were to ever be hurt by you. If you always do that, she'll always wear the smile she's wearing right now. Congratulations to you both and I wish you two well."

I handed the mic to the young man who was taking it around to each of us and sat. Eve mouthed the words thank you and then we ate. When it was all over, Eve asked me and the other sisters to stick around because she had a gift to give us.

Drew, Gerald, and Jared hung around too. They just went to the other side and sat at the bar. We sat at the table and Eve gave us each a gift box. We all opened our boxes at the same time to a cute chain with a pink ribbon as the charm. I was touched by the gift, but we were no longer sisters.

Heaven was the first to speak. "Awww, Eve this is lovely. Thank you."

April was next. "Yes Eve, these are beautiful."

"It is," Keli said putting hers on.

I didn't say anything I just put the lid back on the box. The absolute last thing I needed was for Delilah to say, "So since it ain't green, you don't like it?" she shot at me.

"Delilah, don't start," Eve jumped in quickly.

For Eve I grabbed my purse and stood. "Thank you Eve for the gift. Drew and I will be going now."

"That figures. Maybe if it hadda been green she'd be grateful," Delilah added.

That was it. I threw my purse onto the chair and dove on her ass. I punched her as many times as I could before they pulled me off of her.

Everyone yelling and Delilah trying to get at me had my heart pumping. Then April yelled in my face after pushing me, "Stephanie what's wrong with you? Are you crazy!"

I couldn't control myself, I launched at her and we went down. Drew pulled me off of her and Gerald held on to April. "I hate you trifling bitches and I should have never agreed to come. You have the audacity to sit across from me and talk to me when you know you been fucking my husband," I yelled at April with spit flying from my mouth. I was fuming.

Everyone gasped. "Drew told you that bullshit," she lied.

"No, I figured it out, so don't lie you backstabbing bitch. And you," I turned to Delilah. "He told me about your ho ass. I could care less if the ribbon was green, pink, red or fucking purple because you bitches are not my sisters and I will not be at the wedding tomorrow," I yelled and Drew held on to me tight. Keli and Heaven were speechless and Delilah was just in shock that I knew.

"Fuck you Stephanie," Delilah spat. "No one cares if you come. And yes I fucked Drew. Now you see how that shit feels to have your so-called sister get with your man."

I was in total disbelief. "Drew let me go," I ordered. I marched in Delilah's direction and Keli and Heaven stepped aside. Now that they knew the truth, I assumed they agreed that Delilah deserved whatever I was getting ready to do to her.

I got in her face and she stood up to me, ready for me. "You and Drew never had a relationship Delilah. You liked him and he didn't reciprocate those feelings and you need to get over it. That shit happened in college and you're still singing that same old tired ass song. No matter what games, tricks or schemes you come up with, Drew is my fucking husband! My husband and you will never have my husband, you whore!" I yelled in her face. My eyes filled with tears, as my heart raced. I hated her at that moment and I wanted to rip her head from her shoulders. "After today, I'm done with your ass. Do you hear me, you and April," I spat in her face. I turned to walk away.

"Bitch I was always done with you and I enjoyed every minute of riding Drew's dick," she spat at my back.

I turned back, but Eve stopped me. "Stephanie come on," Eve tugged at my arm. "She's not worth it."

"What? Eve you're taking this bitch's side when you know what she did to me."

Eve turned to her. "Shut up Delilah. Do you not get what you've done? You went too far, you have crossed the line Delilah, and I can't defend you anymore."

I headed to get my purse. Drew reached for me and I snatched away. He wasn't off the hook either. He was still in the dog house with me.

Eve continued, "You and April need to leave. Stephanie and Heaven are the only two I want to stand with me tomorrow and Keli, if she wants to be. You two are no longer welcome to be in my wedding," Eve declared.

Delilah laughed before getting her purse and then said, "I'm good with that. Jared asked me weeks ago to not be in the wedding after he ate my pussy. Right Jared, tell your little Miss Perfect fiancé about that."

Those were the last words out of Delilah's mouth before I saw my Christian friend lose her religion. "You Bitch!" Eve yelled. Then she punched Delilah in her face. They went down and I made my exit. I was no longer interested in what would happen next. I just wanted to get the hell out of there.

In the car Drew tried to comfort me.

"Baby, I'm so, so so——," he tried to say. I cut him off.

I held up my hand. "Don't Drew don't, just take me home." I sniffled. How was I going to forgive him and move on from this? Was all I could wonder, as we rode down the interstate.

Chapter 32

Delilah

What the fuck! I could not believe this shit was going down. Not only did Stephanie's whack ass have the nerve to jump on me, while I was being held back, but Eve had just sucker punched me in my face. Sorority sisters or not both of those bitches had it coming. The heat from Eve's fist had sent me flying back on the marble floor. But there was no way I would fall, oh hell no. I took the full length of my hand and mugged Eve in the face so hard, she flipped over the table. But she had not seen anything yet. I rushed around the table to finish her off.

As I made my way around the table, I went for Eve then Jared pulled me away as I kicked and screamed.

"Get your fucking hands off me!" I bit Jared on his right knuckle. He let go right away and yelled out in agony.

"Damn, why'd you bite me?" He sounded like a wounded kid.

I rolled my eyes at him. "Don't put your hands me on me. Get your fucking fiancée."

"Fuck you Delilah with your nasty ass," Eve spat.

"Yeah whatever bitch. Go home and cry." I straighten my brand new five hundred dollar silk Addie top by Ralph Lauren. These bitches were fucking with my money. These clothes were not made to be fighting in like a hood rat.

Jared tried to help Eve up but she pushed him off. Keli reached out and grabbed her elbow to help her up. They both walked away together trailed by Jared. A pitiful male whore to be honest was not worth my damn time.

Riley walked over and stood next to me. "Are you okay sis," she asked.

I shook my head for yes as I looked around the now almost empty room. I looked at Heaven who stood shaking her head at me in disappointment. Finally without saying a word she turned and exited the room. Then I realized that I didn't see April, she was gone. So was Gerald. I guess they had left. But I knew one thing for sure April was mad at me even though she had my back. She was angry I could see it in her face. Why had I kept all this from her? I sighed.

"Come on let's go," Riley whispered wrapping her arms around my shoulder. Then Keli walked back in, alone and went for her drink on the table and threw it back, as if nothing had happened. Hell to be honest I didn't blame her because this shit was crazy but bound to happen.

Riley walked me to my car then got in hers and sped off to get us some coffee. She would meet me at the house. As I started up my ignition April's name lit up on my cell phone. I hesitated before answering it.

"Just tell me why Delilah?" were April's first words. "Just why?"

I was silent on my end.

"I mean you could have at least told me."

"Look I thought about telling you. But..." Again I grew silent.

"So that's it. You just go behind my back and do some shit."

"This was not about you," I yell.

"Well you know what? It should have been because I feel betrayed."

So now she was the victim. I could not believe this. "April, Drew is not your man. He never was." I regret saying it as soon as it comes out of my mouth.

"Really Delilah. Okay." Next there was the disconnection on the other line. April had ended the call. My heart pounded. Had I ruined our friendship? "Shit," I screamed as I hit my steering wheel.

As soon as I got home I headed straight to the bar. I needed a drink, something straight and strong. A shot glass it was. The drink of choice, Don Julio. This would for sure clear my mind which was exactly what I needed. The first shot I downed burned, but I welcomed it like a beast.

Grabbing the remote I turned on the television and prepared myself for the second round. My mind raced with the replay of the events at the dinner rehearsal. I just could not believe the nerve of Stephanie. That bitch was always at the root of starting shit. Her and that big ass mouth then have the nerve to become the victim in the end. And Drew as I could see was still just her fucking flunky. The both of them could kiss my ass. After my fourth shot of Don Julio I hated Stephanie's ass even more. That bitch refused to give me peace in this life.

But I felt kind of bad for Eve. I had ruined it for her, which I never wanted to do. However, she had asked for it. Why did she always take Stephanie's side? Why was Stephanie always right? Either way I had saved Eve a life of heartache because Jared wasn't shit. And even though she had punched me in my face, I knew she had a good heart and she deserved better.

Hearing Riley's keys jiggling in the door I reach over to pour myself one last shot but almost missed the glass. I'm wasted. That Don Julio had taken effect. One look at my eyes and Riley knew.

"Delilah why are you drinking that poison? Look at you." Riley sat both coffees down and snatched up the Don Julio bottle.

"Hey, what are you doing? That was helping me." My words are a little slurred.

"No that is only temporally making you less delusional. Here drink this."

One sniff of the cup and I knew it was from Chocolate City Coffee Shop. They had the best coffee ever. Forget Starbucks. I took one sip and I was cured, at least that's all I could remember.

Chapter 33

"Hello," I breathed into the phone. I didn't even look at the caller ID to see who it was.

"Are you still asleep?" I noticed the voice right away.

"Duh it's early." I think she must be crazy to be calling so early sounding all up beat.

"Girl it's noon. Get your ass outta bed," Keli declares.

"For real. I feel like I just laid down." I rub my pillow and turn over.

"Well it's late so get up. I was calling to see if you wanted to meet up for lunch so that we can talk."

"Lunch," I repeat. But I knew right away that was not happening my body said it all. "Nah I don't feel like going out. You can stop by if you want to though."

"Alright that's cool. I'll be over in a bit."

"See you then." I agreed then ended the call. Now I had to actually get out of the bed, which I also was not feeling. Tossing back my Donna Karan quilt, I tried to sit up only to be met with a banging headache. Grabbing both of my temples, that Don Julio bottle is the first thing that comes to mind. And here was the payback.

Eventually I was able to get up and take two extra strength Excedrin. I jumped in the shower, washed my face, brushed my teeth then threw on a pink Guess wife beater and some white Guess cut off shorts. I finished just in time because as I headed to the kitchen the doorbell ring. Looking through the peephole I see Keli patiently waiting.

"Hey," I answered the door with a smile as I see Keli holding some much needed food. "Now that's how you show up to someone's house." I joked. Reaching out to help I seize the fruit tray that also had spinach dip and crackers on one side from Keli. In the other hand she was holding a bag.

"Thanks." Keli seemed relieved for the help. "Guess what I have in this bag?"

"Some chicken I hope."

"Try again. Try strawberry milk shakes."

"Dang you must have read my mind." I loved strawberry milk shakes and everyone knew it. "Come on over here." We pulled out chairs to sit down at the table in my den area.

"Where is Riley?"

"Girl she is gone. When I woke up she had split."

Opening up the fruit tray, I grabbed some grapes and put them directly into my watering mouth. I didn't realize how hungry I was into I took my first bite. Next I went for the spinach dip and crackers. I dipped three butter crackers in spinach dip within one minute.

"Damn Delilah, are you starving or nah?" Keli laughed as she watched me devour the food.

"Girl I guess," I laughed. "Thanks for bringing it though." I took a huge gulp from the strawberry shake.

"No problem. Anyway you have got to tell me what's going on. Last night was the craziest I have ever seen it. I still can't believe Eve of all people hit you."

"I know right." I shook my head and reached for more grapes.

"Now that damn ratchet ass Stephanie does not surprise me at all." Keli sipped from her shake.

"Yeah that hoe has been psycho," I cosigned. "But I guess it all just got out of control."

Dipping another cracker and putting it in my mouth whole I decided to spill the beans. Hell, it wasn't doing me any good keeping it all to myself. "Just like Stephanie said I manipulated Drew into sleeping with me."

"But how? I mean why?"

"Keli don't be crazy, you know why. To get back at that bitch Stephanie. Hell I been wanting to get back at her and Drew. I just never knew how. But when I found out that he had been doing April I knew that was my key. I waltzed up in his office and demanded he sleep with me. And of course he tried to deny me at first but that's when I made it clear that if he didn't I would tell Stephanie about him and April."

"So he did it." Keli still seemed shocked. "Hmmph, so how was it?" Keli smiled.

"He was good. At first he tried too hard to pretend he didn't like it. But I put it on his ass so he had no choice once he screamed my name." I knew this was no laughing matter but we both cracked up.

"Damn. You go girl." Keli was enjoying this. And I knew it was all because she too hated Stephanie. This was really what our Sorority sister bond was all about. HATERED. "But Jared what about him?"

210

"Now that was not planned." I looked away as I thought about it. I remembered the day I ran into him as I picked up condoms to go on my first date with Drew. Or should I call it my first forced date with Drew. After that Jared and I ran into each other again and it seemed as though we ran into each other one time too many. "Honestly we just ran in to each other too much and one day it just happened he wanted to keep it going but I put a stop to it. I really felt bad about it because of Eve. I wanted Drew, but his bitch ass kept making excuses and putting me off, so I decided that I was done with him also. Let Stephanie have his weak ass."

"Well, I'm not shocked about Mr. Jared because from what I see he gets around. You know he had started spending a little time at my crib. But he tried to make it seem innocent I guess he thought I might give him some by default. Then he wouldn't have to feel guilty. Though he never asked I knew that's what he wanted but I cut him off too. Eve is better off without his slick cheating ass. But that's also what she gets for always thinking her man shit doesn't stink. He's a nice guy but I never trusted him." I looked at Keli as she spoke she did not care she called it how she seen it. There was no emotion on her face.

"But Stephanie I reveled in her pity last night. Did you see her face she almost cried? She deserves every bit of it. I told her years ago she was wrong for dating Drew. Even if he didn't want to be with you, you were her friend first. Her Sorority Sister. That should have meant something to her but no she never took it serious. Just shit in your face and it made seem like it was no big deal. Sometimes it's just the principal. And the bitch always has the gumption to judge me. Honey please."

Everything Keli said was painfully true. "And I agree with you one hundred and ten percent fuck Stephanie's controlling ass. And Eve we did her gullible ass a favor." I was done and ready to finish my strawberry milkshake.

Chapter 34

Sitting at my desk all morning, I had been trying and I mean trying hard to get some work done. It seemed the harder I tried the more distant my brain had become. Going over a few bank drafts had been all I had been able to accomplish. The only thing I could seem to concentrate on was thinking about April and our friendship. I tried several times, this morning included, to reach her but all my calls and messages went unanswered.

I was starting to believe she would never speak to me again and if that was the case I was going to have to learn to deal with it. But who would I talk to? Riley loved me and we spent time together but mostly she hung out with her friends who I considered to be kids.

Knock, knock. I heard the tap on my office door. "Come in." I mouthed as I straighten up in my seat. While in my deep thoughts I had slouched back in my seat and the last thing I wanted was for the senior VP to visit my office only to find me unglued. Thankfully for me it was only Larissa, my assistant.

"Hey, I was thinking about ordering in for lunch. Would you like for me to order up something for you?"

Looking at the time I notice that it was indeed time for lunch and my stomach growled with confirmation. I had been so deep in thought I hadn't given eating a consideration. Now there would be no denying myself.

"I guess I should. I have no other plans."

"Did you have anything in particular you would like?"

"No what you order will be fine with me."

Larissa looked at me with concern. Stepping completely into the office she turns and closes the door behind her. Without being invited she takes a seat across from me. "Delilah are you okay?"

I almost said I was fine but Larissa had been working with me for a long time. I think it was safe to say that she knew when something was bothering me. I decided not to give her the I'm fine speech but I would still keep her at bay. "You know just stressing over what went down with me and my sorority sisters. Now that the wedding is off and half of us not speaking to one another. I just don't know how we will make amends." I said really only caring about me and April. I didn't give a fuck about the rest of them evil bitches.

"It will all work out, don't worry. It will take some time. They will come around." She encouraged. She gave me a bright smile and went back to her desk. A few moment later there was another knock.

"Come in." Again it was Larissa.

"Ummm, April just called and said that she will meet you for lunch."

"I…um…okay," I say shocked but trying to conceal it. "Tell her I will be there in drive time."

"Will do. I guess I don't need to order in lunch for you," Larissa smiled before closing my door.

Grabbing my purse, I headed straight out. I had called April this morning and left her a message that I wanted to meet up at Jack Daniels for lunch. But just like my other calls and messages it went unanswered. I guess she had a change of heart.

April was already seated when I arrived but I noted that she had not ordered a drink which normally was her first order of business. I felt a few butterflies in the pit of my stomach. For as far back as I could remember our friendship had never been in this space with each other, it was always with the other girls.

"Hey," I spoke first as soon as I approached the table.

"Hey," April tossed back.

I tried to read her facial expression but no answers were there. "I'm glad you agreed to meet me. I've been calling you."

"I've been busy."

"Too busy to answer my calls? Because if that's so, this is a first." Again there I went putting my foot in my mouth. I looked away for a brief moment. "Look, I'm sorry."

"It's cool Delilah. I just need to know why you would not tell me. And this has nothing to do with Drew. Fuck him. I could care less about him or what you did with him. It's just the secret, the going behind my back that bothers me. We are supposed to be better than that."

She was right. "I know how I went about it was wrong. You're right. I should have kept it real with you, but the reason I didn't tell you is because I thought you would try to talk me out of it and that is the last thing I wanted. You see April, all the pain and deceit that I have carried for Drew and Stephanie for years has been brewing. I have never forgiven them, especially her, and you know that. So when I saw this chance to get back at her I took it and I didn't want anything to stand in the way. I never meant to hurt you or deceive you. Our friendship means more than that to me."

"I know you didn't. I've just been being silly over this whole thing," April releases. "I have missed you like crazy these last couple of days. With no one to talk to it has been hell." She grinned for the first time.

"I know. Keli came by the other day to visit with me."

"Yeah I know. She called me too. We talked but I still can't talk to anyone like I can talk with you."

I felt the same way so I guess we both had been suffering.

"Do you know that Gerald stopped talking to me or maybe I should say he broke up with me? Some shit about 'how could I sleep with my best friend's husband?' I told him that bitch ain't my best friend we are sorority sisters and there's a difference. Any who he went on to question whether I had slept with Drew while he and I were dating. He said either way he could not trust me and that he was done. Can you believe that shit?" April looked she would cry.

"Wow," was all I could manage. I knew how much she had started to care for Gerald.

"And it's all because of that bitch Stephanie. Couldn't she have waited for another time to do that shit? Didn't she see my man was with me and that maybe he didn't need to hear all that? That's why I'm not sorry I slept with Drew. That bitch is evil."

"She never cares who she hurts but let's have a drink and toast to her divorce," I smiled.

"Divorce? That bitch ain't divorcing Drew. According to Heaven they started counseling last week and are trying to work it out. Guess she ain't gone let us break up her fake ass happy home."

"After the big show she put on." I was feeling some type of way about this bit of information. For some reason I felt like Stephanie was still trying to get back at me. Show me that Drew would always and forever be hers. I sighed. "And Eve's stupid. How she gone take up for Stephanie when she ruined her wedding? Because if Stephanie had been a true friend, she would have waited to bring all that shit up. But no, as usual, that hoe was thinking about herself."

"I agree but you know what my conclusion is for now. FUCK THEM BOTH!!

"And I will drink to that," I laughed. With that I signaled the waitress to our table. "Bring us both a margarita and quick."

"That's right it's turn up time. It's been a minute," April sang.

***

April and I had a six hour lunch and I enjoyed every minute of it. The office would have to wait until tomorrow. When I got home I wanted to relax so after heading upstairs I drew myself a hot bath, lit some candles, and climbed in. And that is where I stayed for the next two hours catching up on my book by Anna Black titled Now You Wanna Come Back 2. I relaxed mind, body, and soul by the time I climbed out.

Once out of the tub though my mind slowly drifted back to Stephanie. I despised the way she lived her life, believing that it would always be perfect. I mean who forgives a man who sleeps with two of her sorority sisters and lies about it. The chick was either psycho or really trying to win the game. But this time around

I would not be the underdog. Looking at my body in the full length mirror I smiled. This time I would checkmate, that much was clear. Throwing on some PJ's I prepared to go downstairs to grab myself a night snack because I was feeling a little hungry. I also felt like finding a good movie that would help me doze off. Looking at the clock on my nightstand I noticed that it was almost 10pm and Riley still was not home.

Seeing a light flash in the den eased my mind that Riley was pulling up. Heading on into the kitchen I reach in the fridge and grab some fresh strawberries I had picked up from Kroger the day before. I also grabbed the whipped cream. I licked my lips thinking of the goodness this snack would bring. After washing off the strawberries Riley still had not come inside. I wondered what was keeping her. Walking in the den I looked outside and noticed an unknown car pulled in behind Riley car.

Concerned I opened the front door and came face to face with Riley locked in a heated kiss. My presence stalled them and they parted looking me dead in the face he spoke.

"Hey Delilah." Shocked I looked from him to Riley and walked away. How could he speak to me like that was okay.

I hear Riley tell him goodnight then I hear the front door shut. Angry, I stop and face her.

"How could you Riley? You met Gerald before so you knew that he dated April. Hell, they just broke up a week ago."

"I know that Delilah you don't have to remind me." She had the nerve to get smart. "That gives you no reason to be rude."

"Rude. Is that all you care about?" I looked at her like she was crazy. "That was April's man Riley. April. You do remember her don't you? She's only my best friend," I said in a sarcastic tone.

218

"You said it. She is your friend, not mine."

"What?" I yell.

Riley looks away for a minute then turns and looks back at me. This time she looks more rational. "Look I'm sorry..." she stalls. "I didn't mean for any of this to happen. The night that all that mess went down I went to the coffee shop to pick up the coffee and Gerald happened to be there. He was really upset after finding out about April. I sat down with him for a couple of minutes to try and calm him down. We ended exchanging numbers and we just kinda started talking. We have a lot in common."

"Well, you have to break it off with him and soon. April cannot find out about this."

"Did you hear what I just said? We like each other Delilah."

"Riley who cares you can't date him," I yelled at her. "Now just end it. He'll bounce back trust me." I turned and headed toward the kitchen. Picking up the whipped cream I start to put it on my strawberries. Riley comes in the kitchen.

"All you care about is your friend. But I am your sister." I could see tears forming in her eyes so I try not to make eye contact with her.

"I know that and I care about you, but what would it look like, my sister dating my best friend's ex-boyfriend?"

"Hah well ain't that the pot calling the kettle black. Was it not you and April who just slept with your sorority sisters' men?"

My head shot up. If looks could kill, Riley would have dropped dead. I could not believe she had said that.

"You know what? Kiss my ass Riley. I'm going to bed." I snatch my bowl of strawberries off the counter and walk past Riley then turn to face her. "Now you end it or else."

"Don't threaten me Delilah. You never have my back."

"Never have your back? How dare you! I was the one who raised you, loved you, and fed you." I threw back as a matter of fact.

"You're right and you know what, I will end it so that you can keep your precious friendship since that's all you care about. You live and breathe your friend, but what about your own mother? You won't sacrifice nothing to fix your relationship with her."

"Fuck that. There ain't nothing to fix. Besides she's the one who broke the family. So she is the one who should fix it. She is the one who left us on our own remember?" Tears swelled in my both my eye sockets and cascaded down my cheeks. "I was a child." I took the back of my right hand and wiped the tears so that I could see again.

"Now you end it." I was done.

Chapter 35

CHECKMATE

It had been three weeks since the blow up and the whole time I had thought of nothing more. No matter how I tried to clear my mind of it I couldn't. It taunted me like a bump. I had to be rid of it. So out of all of my anguish I built up the nerve to call up Heaven. Even though I had done nothing to her personally she had not reached out to me. It was no secret that she was not happy with the outcome of Stephanie's story of me. Subsequently I was amazed when I called her up and she did not hang up in my face. Nevertheless, I knew that she would be the only one that would be able to help me.

And finally the time was here. It had took me almost a week to convince Heaven to pull the girls, along with their men, together for one last time. I told her I would get April to come since we were back on good terms. Also April would be the only one besides Heaven that would know that we would be attending. I mean who was I kidding, the other girls would never show up if they knew that we would be there. I mean all with the exception of Keli.

At first when I told April she flat out refused but eventually agreed. I told her what time to arrive. This way we would make our grand entrance together. For once and for all, I wanted to clear the air.

I pulled up to Heaven's at the same time as April so she was on time. Turning off my ignition I looked around and noticed that everyone that I was expecting to be here was indeed inside judging from the vehicles.

"Are you really ready to go inside with those sea monsters?" April referred to the girls as she approached me.

"As ready as I will ever be and ain't no turning back now."

"I guess not we're here. So let's go." April looked towards the door. I started walking and she fell into step beside me.

Reaching the front door I prepared to ring the doorbell. "Here goes nothing." I pushed the button. In no time flat Heaven opened the door.

"What's up y'all?" She spoke as if this was normal gathering. Well I guess you could say it was because our gathering lately had all been full of drama.

"Nothing," I replied. "Do they know it's us?"

"Nope," was Heaven only reply. "Come on in."

Following behind Heaven, we entered her den where we came face to face with Stephanie, Drew, Eve, and Keli. Although Keli was sitting on a sofa alone she didn't seem to be at battle with anyone. She smiled at us and spoke.

"Heaven, what the fuck are they doing here?" Eve roared.

I was so shocked to hear those words come out of Eve mouth I did a double take. Damn, she had turned into a straight up sinner. I almost laughed. I guess we had ruined her life.

"For real Heaven because I don't have time for this shit. My husband and I…" Stephanie said looking directly at me like I was the only one in the room. "Don't have time for this we have moved on."

Although she was still being a bitch I would have expected her reaction to be worse than Eve's.

"Look I asked you ladies here tonight for a reason. We are sorority sisters and that is a tie that will forever bind us together. We took vows, almost like a marriage, of sisterhood, to be there for each other; to love and protect one another, and lift each other up. But all we have managed to do is tear each other apart. There just has to be something we can do to fix this. Especially if some of us are willing.

DING DONG! The doorbell chimed.

Heaven must have been expecting someone because the look on everyone else's face was surprise. Heaven excused herself while she went to answer the door. Following close behind on her heels when she returned was Jared.

"Oh hell no. I'm out." Eve stood to leave but Heaven jumped in front of her.

"No Eve, just sit down for a minute and listen. Jared just wanted a chance to apologize to you. He knows he screwed up."

"I just can't right now." Tears streamed down Eve's face as her body went limp and she fell back down into her seat. "I just can't."

"Look I will go." Jared turned to leave.

"No," Heaven said. "Stay for a moment Jared. Like I was saying earlier some of us are at least willing to fix this maybe one day we can get back to the way it used to be."

"I see what you are trying to do Heaven but it is way past that now. Honestly, I feel offended that you would even invite us into the same house as these whores." She pointed in April and my direction.

Instead of popping off I smiled and chilled.

"I mean Drew how do you feel being in the same room with someone who manipulated you into sleeping with them? I mean it's really disgusting."

"Babe we don't need to justify nothing here. It's like you said, we are working on us. All this is old news." Drew stood. "Sweetie let's just go."

I had heard enough of these fake shenanigans it was time to get down to business. "Actually Drew if you don't mind could you have a seat for just a brief moment and I promise we will clear all this up so that no one in this room is mistaken or should I say misinformed. April if you want you can go ahead and grab a drink then maybe a seat." April looked at me, grinned, and then went to have a seat next to Keli.

"Now I asked Heaven to bring all of you here tonight because I think there is a misconception here. I've been called whores, bitches, and all those horrible names, which I really believe are a bit redundant.

"Drew and Stephanie I commend you two on trying to keep your family together. I'm all for family sticking together. You see when I was coming up I didn't have a mother or a father. My family was a bit dysfunctional but that is neither here or there. The point is I applaud you for staying a strong family. Which should make it that much easier for you to welcome the new addition to your family." I rubbed my stomach.

Keli who had just took a swallow of her drink almost choked. April patted her in the back to make sure she was okay.

Stephanie looked at Drew than back at me as if she was confused so I needed to be matter of fact. "That's right, I'm pregnant and it's yours Drew!" I looked Stephanie straight in the eyes. "Checkmate!"

"Drew tell me you didn't sleep with her unprotected?"

"Babe I didn't. She's lying I used protection."

"Yeah we did," I spoke up. "But all three times I punched a hole inside. See I'm sneakier than you."

"Wait a minute…three times? Drew you told me you only slept with her once." Stephanie slapped him in the face and spit flew out of his mouth.

"Well honey he lied to you. Tell her Drew. Tell her you even called my name." I taunted her, lying about the number of times.

"Stephanie, baby she is lying. It was only once!" he cried.

"I'll kill you this time bitch." Stephanie jumped in my direction but Heaven and Jared grabbed her.

"Let's go Stephanie. I promise you this is the last time I will ever be in the same room with this nasty trifling bitch," Eve yelled. "And Heaven the next time you try and have a reunion I will cut you off too." Eve grabbed her purse. "Let Stephanie go. It would serve the bitch right if Stephanie killed her. Come on Jared." She grabbed him by the arm.

I no longer felt bad for Eve since she had so much to say tonight. "Eve you have a lot of words tonight. It's funny that you call me nasty and maybe you are right since I did Jared in your house in your bed. Did you forget to tell her that Jared?"

Eve world look like it fell apart at that moment. "In my house Jared, where I lay my head?" Eve went for the lamp on the table closest to her and threw it at Jared. It missed his head only by an inch. Turning on his heels, he hauled ass for the door as Keli grabbed Eve and pulled her down on the couch. Appearing around the corner from the front door were Gerald and Riley holding hands. The courage I was wearing on my shoulders suddenly fell as I turned and looked at April.

"What the hell is this Gerald?" He said nothing. "Riley," she asked next.

The room grew silent as April looked to me last for answers. "Delilah what is this?"

My eyes roamed Gerald and Riley who had left it up to me. "I was going...She was supposed to brea—"

"So you knew about this." April eyes were once again full of betrayal that I had caused.

I was speechless.

April rushed out the door and I knew our friendship was over. I went after her and yelled her name but she jumped in her car and burned rubber. Turning around, I saw Riley standing in the driveway along with Gerald. I could not believe she had shown up with him knowing April would be there.

At home, I fell on the couch so that I could think. Drinking was out. I was done with that until after the baby. Everything inside of me told me to put Riley's ass out. I could not believe her. But I didn't have the energy so instead I decided to go to bed. Climbing the stairs I hear Riley rush in the house calling my name.

"Leave me alone," I yell.

"Delilah, Delilah," I could now hear the tears in Riley's voice.

"What?" I turn around and face her as she stood at the bottom of the stairs.

"It's Mom. I just got a call from the hospital she has been in a horrible accident and she's on life support."

"What?" I let out a cry from my soul. The room swayed as I blacked out.

Chapter 36

Keli

"Wow! And to think, I've been called all those names and yet I'm the only one who hasn't slept with anyone's man."

"Uh, excuse you. You slept with Quinton," Heaven said.

"Uh, excuse you; he wasn't your man boo and I thought you had met someone else anyway. Why are you still stuck on his broke ass?"

"I'm not stuck on him. It's just the fact that you did."

"And the fact still remains I had him first so technically you were the one he was cheating with."

"What about you and Jared?" Eve asked in between sobs.

"What about me and Jared? I never slept with him and I've never wanted to. I told you that morning at my house that Jared and I are friends and that's it. I didn't know he was fooling around with Delilah."

"What the fuck is going on around here? What ever happened to our friendship, our sorority ties? Didn't they mean anything?" Stephanie said walking back into Heaven's living room.

"Hold up!" I said standing up. "Now you want to cry about sorority ties when you all have never treated me like a sister. All you do is talk about me, call me names, and expect me to sleep with your men but look at you now. It's amazing, absolutely fucking amazing!" I laughed.

"What's amazing? There isn't anything that has happened tonight that is funny Keli," Stephanie said.

"Yes it is. Look at you Stephanie. Ms. My Shit Don't Stink Like Yours. You walk around here with your nose up in the air like no one is on your level. You acted like your home was better than anybody's when it's a mess too. You put your man so high up on a pedestal that not even your ass can reach him now. You scheduled when to have sex with the man for God's sake and you wonder why he went running to April's ass, who probably did anything he asked her to do."

"That's enough Keli," Heaven screamed.

"No it's not. Look at my little angel Eve. Did you honestly think Jared wouldn't have sex before getting married? Do you not remember meeting him at a party? Be for real. You had blinders on and you were too busy trying to make sure you didn't slip up in front of your sorority sisters that you didn't see what was happening in front of your own eyes."

"So I'm to blame?" Eve asked.

"Not for the things Jared did. But for allowing yourself to be stupid, yes."

"And who are you to know anything? You're—"

"Ratchet and ghetto?" I said finishing Stephanie's sentence. "Well let me tell you what I do know. I know that I am a well-educated African American woman with a home and two cars that are paid for. I have more money in the bank than all of you put together and when I place myself into friendships I value them for the long haul but neither of you girls would look at me long enough to see that. All y'all wanted to see was the Keli that could get down with the best of them but nothing else."

"Girl, go on with all that. I don't have time to worry about your little feelings when my entire house has blown up in my face. My fucking husband has a baby on the way by that skank ass Delilah and you want me to be concerned about your feelings, not today."

"Look Keli, we only saw what you portrayed so don't blame us for treating you like you've always acted."

"Really Heaven? You really think I wanted to be dogged by my friends, my so called sisters, whenever you all felt like it? Y'all didn't care where we were or what you said. Did any of you stop to take my feelings into account? You think I wanted that? You really think I wanted to be the one thought of as a home wrecker when I've never done that. Yes, I've slept around but never with a married man and never, ever with anyone associated with any of you. Yet I'm always the one to blame."

"What more do you want from us Keli? Do you want us to apologize? What?" Eve shouted.

I laughed. "You know what, I only came today because Heaven called me but after everything we've been through I can honestly say that I am done. I hope and pray that each of you find the happiness you deserve but I'm done. After today, I'm cutting the ties," I said grabbing my purse to leave.

I smiled walking to my car and for the first time in a long time, I was actually leaving with a smile on my face. I got in my car and headed straight to Delilah's. That heifer had some explaining to do.

When I knocked on the door, she came looking like she had aged 10 years.

"What in the hell happened to you?"

"My mom was in an accident."

"Oh my God, is she okay?"

"I don't know and I thought I didn't care, but I do. Keli my mom was never a mother and I had to grow up fast and raise Riley. I mean, why should I even care about her now when she never cared about me? I thought I hated her until now."

"Because she is still your mom Delilah and no matter what happened, you'd never want her to die. Has she changed?"

"I guess. I wouldn't have anything to do with her and now I don't know if I'll have the chance."

"Do you want me to take you to the hospital?"

"Not yet. I'm not ready to see her like that. I'm going to wait on Riley to call me with an update and then I will decide. Anyway, what are you doing here?"

"Well, I was coming to shake your motherfucking hand but after all this…"

"Shaking my hand? Why?" She asked slumping back down on the couch.

"Are you serious Delilah? You've been sleeping with Jared and Drew and now you're pregnant."

"Yea, well both of those stuck up bitches deserved it and the look on their faces, priceless! I only wish now I could have a drink to celebrate."

"Girl, you are crazy. I can't say that ruining a home is what anyone deserves but karma is a bitch."

"Yep and we are best friends."

"So, when are you going to tell them the truth?" I asked no longer laughing.

"The truth about what?"

"The baby's father."

"What are you talking about? Drew is the baby's father."

"Come on Delilah, you should know me better than that. We both know that neither Drew nor Jared is that baby's father because you aren't really pregnant."

"Get the fuck out of my house Keli."

"Why the rush? Did I hit a nerve?" I smiled.

"You didn't hit shit but you're about to get hit if you don't leave now."

"You wouldn't even attempt to hit me because you don't want the ass whooping that comes along with that."

"I'm not going to ask you again to leave my house."

"After you tell the truth."

"I don't have to tell you anything. Who do you think you are?"

"I think I am the one that is about to blow your plans up in smoke. Now, do you want to break the news to Drew or shall I?"

"What news?" Drew asked walking in. "What is she talking about Delilah?"

"What are you doing here Drew?"

"I got a text that said to come so here I am."

"You can thank me later," I said to Drew.

"What is going on?" Drew asked again.

"Since she won't tell you, I will. Delilah isn't pregnant."

"Shut up Keli!" She screamed.

"She can't have children. She had an accident when we were in college that left her incapable of getting pregnant. Nobody knew but me because I walked in her hospital room when the doctor was breaking the news to her and her parents."

"She's lying." Delilah yelled.

"Are you serious?" Drew asked charging at her.

"Get your fucking hands off of me Drew!"

"You ruined my family and you're not even pregnant. Oh my God! I cannot believe this shit is even happening!"

"I didn't ruin your raggedy ass family, you did; you sorry bastard. And yes I am pregnant regardless if you believe it or not. You knew that I was interested in you but you walked all over me with that bitch Stephanie and you want me to feel sorry about ruining your life. Fuck you! Fuck you Drew!"

"How could I have been so stupid to fall for your tricks? I should have just let you tell Stephanie about me and April from the beginning but instead I made the mistake of sleeping with you. Damn it!"

"It wasn't a mistake! It wasn't a mistake. You loved every minute of it especially when you were calling my name. Admit it, you were in love with this pussy," she said walking up to him.

"Don't touch me!" Drew said pushing her away from him. "I don't love anything about your crazy psychotic ass. You tried to ruin my life and for what? Did you think I would come running to you once Stephanie left?"

"Yes and you would have if it was not for her!" She said pointing at Keli. "I told you to get the fuck out my house bitch!"

"Shit! I've got to find Stephanie. Delilah, don't you ever contact me or my wife again or I will have your ass arrested. I mean it."

"Don't leave me Drew! DREW! Don't leave me!" She screamed after him falling to the floor. "Why are you doing this Keli? What have I ever done to you?" She asked with tears in her eyes. "And you are wrong everything you said is wrong."

Grabbing my purse, I simply smile and reply, "I'm Karma."

"For your sake you better hope she's right, Drew." I heard Delilah scream from the background but I was done.

Chapter 37

"Hey."

"Hey yourself. When did you get here?"

"About an hour ago. You were sleeping so peacefully that I didn't want to wake you."

"You know I don't mind you waking me," I said pulling him in for a kiss.

"Hmm, you taste good even with morning breath," he said climbing on top of me as I pulled his shirt over his head.

"I've missed you."

"Have you?"

"Yea, can't you tell?" I asked sliding his hand down to my girl who was wet and hot.

"Damn girl! I can get used to waking up to this."

"So can I, now stop talking," I said pushing his head down under the cover. "Yes baby, just like that." I moaned as he took me into his mouth. He was taking his time savoring my lady and I was enjoying every minute.

"Oh, baby; I need you now!" I moaned as I pulled him up.

"You want this? You sure you want this?"

"Boy, if you don't stop playing." I said wrapping my legs around him as he entered me.

"Hmm, you feel so good," he grunted.

"Don't stop!" I screamed grabbing his ass.

"Slow down, I ain't going nowhere." He said slowing down as he pulled out and pushed back in.

"Oh God!" I screamed.

"How does it feel?"

"It feels good!"

"You want me to stop?"

"No, please don't stop. Oh, I'm cum'ing!"

"Uh, uh," he groaned as his pace increased and my legs got tighter around him. "Shit girl!"

Collapsing on me, I wiped the sweat from my forehead. "Now that's what you call a wakeup call."

"What do you have planned before we leave for vacation?"

"Nothing other than getting my nails and feet done. I've already packed and can't wait to leave. Spending seven days in paradise with you is all I need right now."

"I so agree. Have you heard from any of the girls lately?"

"No and I don't care to really. My life has been stress free and I'm loving it," I said as my phone vibrated. "This is my assistant."

"I'm going to take a shower while you get that. Come join me when you're done."

"Hey Shea, what's up?"

"Hey boss lady. There's a Stephanie here to see you. I told her that you were on vacation but she wouldn't leave until I called you."

"What do she want?"

"I don't know. I have her sitting in the reception area. Do you want to talk to her?"

"No. Take her number and tell her I will call her when I get back from vacation."

"Gotcha! Have fun and bring me something back."

"Don't I always? Hold down the fort until I return."

"Don't I always?"

"Thanks Shea." As soon as I hang up the phone to join my man in the shower, I hear another phone vibrating on the night stand. Picking it up, I see the name on the caller ID and I smile.

"Jared, your phone is ringing."

Chapter 38

"Hey, how was the vacation?"

"Shea it was great. Man! I didn't want to come back and—"

"OH MY GOD!" Shea screamed. "Is that a ring on your finger?"

"Well dang! You didn't give me a chance to tell you," I smiled.

"Tell me what? What is it?"

"Well…"

"Well what? Come on, spit it out!"

"Okay! Calm down lil momma."

"Dammit boss lady, if you don't tell me now," she screamed.

"Yes, we got married while in Jamaica."

"I knew it! Was it planned?"

"No, I had no idea he was even thinking about marriage, but I love him and he loves me and he makes me happy."

"I'm so happy for you guys! Does anyone else know?"

"Only his family. You know I don't really have anybody but you and now you know."

"Well, I am so happy for you. You so deserve this happiness."

"Thank you Shea. I never thought I would be this happy but I am." I told her as I heard a knock on my door.

"Stephanie?" I said confused when I saw her standing at the door.

"Sorry but there was no one at the reception desk."

"What can I do for you?"

"Can I talk to you?"

"I'll bring your coffee and schedule. Can I get you something to drink Stephanie?"

"Juice would be good, if that's okay."

"Sure thing."

"What's up Stephanie? I wasn't expecting you to show up here. I said I would call you when I got back from vacation."

"Keli, look; I didn't come here to fight with you. After everything that has gone on, it's the last thing I need," she said as Shea came back with the coffee, juice and my schedule.

"Thanks Shea. Give me 30 minutes and then I'll be ready to go over my schedule."

"Sure thing boss lady."

"Okay Stephanie, tell me why you're here?"

"I came here to apologize to you. I am so sorry for all the things I put you through. I was selfish and you didn't deserve it."

"Wow. I don't think I've ever heard you apologize for anything. Wow."

"I know but I truly am sorry. It took me almost losing my family to understand that."

"You said almost. So are you and Drew still together?"

"Yes, it's been a struggle, but after I found out that Delilah was lying about being pregnant we continued on through counseling and we've recommitted ourselves to each other. It's been hard but I love Drew and he's all I've ever known."

"I'm glad to hear that and I do wish you all much happiness."

"Thank you. It means a lot. We really do miss you, you know? All the girls miss you."

"Yea, that's good to know. Hard to believe but good to know. How is everyone doing?"

"Heaven is getting married to Miguel, the guy she met at her clinic and Eve accepted her calling to ministry and is over the single's ministry at her church."

"That's great. What about April and Delilah?"

"I've talked to April and we are on the road to amends but it's not 100% yet. Her mom is sick and she moved her into her home so she is spending all of her time taking care of her. I haven't talked to Delilah and I have no desire to yet. I know I have to forgive her too but it's so hard."

"But you forgave Drew, didn't you? I understand Drew is your husband and the father of your children but they couldn't have done anything without his participation."

"I know but Keli, they were supposed to be my sisters. April has apologized, but Delilah still thinks I deserved what she did. Can you believe that?"

"I'm not surprised. Delilah has always felt like Drew was meant for her. I hope she gets some help."

"Me too, but I am not going to take up anymore of your time. I know it's been a while since we've spoken and it didn't end on good terms but I had to apologize. And it's sad that we've been friends all these years and this is my first time being at your new office. It looks great and I am so proud of you. I saw your new billboard."

"Thanks. I am proud of the things I've accomplished. I just opened my second insurance office downtown."

"That's great Keli. I wish you nothing but success. Here is my card. If you ever feel like getting together with us again, call me."

"Thanks. I'll think about it."

After being back at work for a full day after vacation, it seems like the day took forever to end. I was meeting Jared for dinner and I couldn't wait to fill him in on my conversation with Stephanie.

"Hey babe, have you been waiting long?"

"No, I just got here."

"Right this way," the hostess said.

On the way to our table, I heard someone call Jared's name. I continued on to the table but he reached out to stop me. Turning around we came face to face with Eve.

"Keli? Are you and Jared dating now?"

"No," I answered.

"Oh, I just thought because I saw you two together," she said.

"We're not dating, we're married," Jared corrected her.

"Married? Really, um, I'm happy for you two."

"Isn't lying a sin?" I asked.

"Eve, I'm sorry things didn't work out between us," Jared said.

"Me too. I really wish that things could have been different for us but I guess God had other plans."

"I guess He did. I tried to tell you I never slept with Delilah but you were so hell bent on believing everyone else but me and when it all finally came out, it was too late. You're a great woman and I know you will make an even greater wife, but it just wasn't meant for us to be together."

"You're right and I have no ill feelings against either of you and I wish you all the best."

"We wish the same for you."

"I guess today is the day for reunions."

"What do you mean?"

"Stephanie came to see me today."

"Really, what did she want?"

"To apologize."

"Wait, Stephanie apologized?"

"Yes, can you believe it? She apologized for the way she treated me."

"Well that's a start. Do you ever think you can be friends with them again?"

"I don't know babe. Those girls were something else. I know that I wasn't a saint, but I didn't deserve to be treated like trash by them either."

"I agree but you all have a bond that you share and if it can be saved then it's worth a try."

"I hear you and I'll think about it, but right now I want to enjoy dinner with my husband."

Chapter 39

"Dearly Beloved, we are gathered together here in the sign of God – and in the face of this company – to join together this man and this woman in holy matrimony, which is commended to be honorable among all men; and therefore – is not by any – to be entered into unadvisedly or lightly – but reverently, discreetly, advisedly and solemnly. Into this holy estate these two persons present now come to be joined. If any person can show just cause why they may not be joined together – let them speak now or forever hold their peace."

"Heaven, you look gorgeous."

"Thank you Keli. I am so glad you and Jared could make it."

"We wouldn't have missed it, Mrs. Heaven Rivera."

"Can you believe it? I's married now!" she laughed.

"Yes you are and you made a beautiful bride," Eve said walking up. "Hey Keli, you look great."

"Thanks Eve and so do you. Where did Stephanie and April go?"

"Here we are," Stephanie said. "We went to change out of those bridesmaids dresses."

"Oh, don't act like they were that bad."

"They weren't, thank God. And you'll be happy to know I didn't have anything green."

"Wait, no green? You want me to believe that Stephanie, the queen of green didn't have anything on her green? Yea right."

"It's true, I promise. I told you I was growing." She laughed.

"And you aren't the only one," April said rubbing my stomach.

"I know right. Three more months and I can have my body back because a sister is tired," I laughed.

"Well ladies, I am truly glad that you all are here. I know that we've had a rough year, but we made it back to each other and I am so happy about that. I know that we are still missing Delilah but the fact that all of you have showed up for me; there are no words."

"Has anyone heard from Delilah?"

"I talked to her last month and she was still thinking about coming so I was surprised she didn't show up. She did move to Dallas after her mom passed away and Riley got married and she seems to be doing really well for herself. She wouldn't talk about the relationship she was in but she seems happy and I told her that I wished her the best," Heaven said.

"That's good to hear. I too wish her the best," I told them. "She still hasn't forgiven me for telling Drew the truth."

"I am glad you did. It was because of you that we were able to get our shit together," Stephanie added.

"I couldn't let her go through with that because she was taking it too far and then to find out she lied about sleeping with Jared. I mean she really had me believing her. I can say that it was because of that lie that we ended up together and I've never been happier. I'm sorry Eve if it hurts to hear that."

"No, it's cool. I realized that I was rushing things with Jared and had we gotten married, it probably wouldn't have lasted so I am glad you two found each other. Jared wasn't the one for me," she replied.

"Isn't it crazy how everything has turned out?"

"Yea, I mean our lives have all taken different turns and even through some ups and some major downs we all manage to end up here celebrating Heaven's wedding."

"I know because had you asked me a year ago, I would have probably laughed in your face but I am happy that we are all here now," I told them.

"Yea, life is funny that way."

"Here," Stephanie said passing everyone a drink. I already had a glass of water. "To the Sorority Ties that bind us together forever as sisters. I pray that we always find our way back to one another, no matter where we go and what we go through! I love you girls!"

"Forever together through the smiles we'll share and the tears we've cried; may we always share the bond of our Sorority Ties."

Chapter 40

Today had not been my day from start to finish. All the planning I had done trying to surprise Heaven at her wedding was a bust. And I swear I had plans on giving Jet Airlines the business once I made it back to Dallas. Never in the history of me flying had my flight ever been delayed three times in one day. Unbelievable.

Then I get to the hotel only to find out my luggage had not been delivered yet so I had to run down to Macy's to find something to wear. It was crazy but finally I made it. Yeah the wedding was over but hey I was in just enough time for the real party the reception. As my driver pulled in front of Towers Reception Hall I noted the limousine Escalade truck and all the vehicles parked out front. It confirmed that it was already going down.

As the car came to a slow yet comfortable halt my driver, Marvin, got out and came around on my side and opened the door. Yes I had a driver. Dallas had been good to me. After moving there and reconciling with mother, before she passed. I went right back to work although I had to take some time off. They had been impressed from the start and immediately after returning to work I landed a position as Senior President at one of Dallas' most prestigious banks. With that being said, I didn't miss my sorority sisters at all. April maybe, but that's it. I still had love for her. She was my girl. Smiling I looked down at my new revamped body that was fresh out of the gym. Damn I looked good after the changes in my life and Marvin eyes could not seem to leave my body confirmed all my thoughts.

Upstaging was clearly what I did best but no drama today or at least I hoped. Again I grinned to myself. I had some unfinished business to attend to, like attending Heaven's most precious day, her wedding day.

Putting my hand on the door knob I prepared to see the people in my life that once made my world go around. As I opened the door the sight was beautiful in the Towers from the looks of it Heaven's theme was Paris. It was gorgeous and my heart fluttered at the sight. And there at the front of the room surrounded by all the visitors were my sorority sisters toasting in a silence filled room.

All eyes were now on me. I almost felt uncomfortable until I was snapped out of it. "Wait Lil Drew come back here," I yelled to my eleven-month-old son who had just started walking. I had been holding his little had, but while I was in awe he had broken free.

At the call of his name I heard a glass crack. Looking to the left of me for a brief second I noticed it was Drew. I smiled but instantly shot off behind my son. Ironically he ran right to April and she scooped him up as I approached.

"Sorry." I didn't know he would break out like that I laughed.

"Awww Delilah, he so cute." April kissed him on the cheek and Lil Drew grinned.

"Wait now what did you call him?" Stephanie asked.

"We call him Lil Drew," I confirmed still smiling at my son as he hugged April he loved her from first sight.

All eyes were of course still glued to me.

"Buttt why…"she paused. "Why would you call him that?" Stephanie said almost like she had a rock in her throat her words were cracking.

"Stephanie now is not the time." Looking at Heaven I noticed she looked beautiful. "Congratulations Heaven." I reached out and gave her a hug.

"Thanks for coming Delilah." Heaven was pleasant.

"No problem I tried not to miss the wedding but my flight was canceled three times. It was a mess."

"But you made it," April said clearly happy to see me. She could care less what my son was called, unlike some people. Eve eyes burned a hole through me but I was still the bitch that did not care.

"You know what Heaven I don't mean to ruin your wedding but this right here." Stephanie shook her head. "Drew," she all of a sudden yelled. "Drew," she screamed again.

"Yeah baby." He made his way over daring himself not to look in my direction.

"You better tell me something. I thought you said this was not your baby. Hell I thought she wasn't even pregnant."

"Well that's what Keli said." Drew looked at Keli whose face was expressionless.

"Keli," Stephanie wanted an answer.

"Look, that's what I thought."

"No bitch that is what you assumed, but you were wrong."

"And since you are so interested Stephanie, my son's name is Drew and yes he is a junior. I named him, that's right, after his dad." I turned to Drew then I reached for my son.

"All this time I have been listening to you. I knew I would never be able to trust you bitch. " Stephanie reached out and punched Keli. Keli grabbed Stephanie's hair and they went to the floor. Grabbing my son I headed for the door. This shit would never end and to be honest I loved it. And these bitches still didn't know the half. I laughed inside.

"Wait Delilah, I'm coming with you." April raced after me.

Also Available

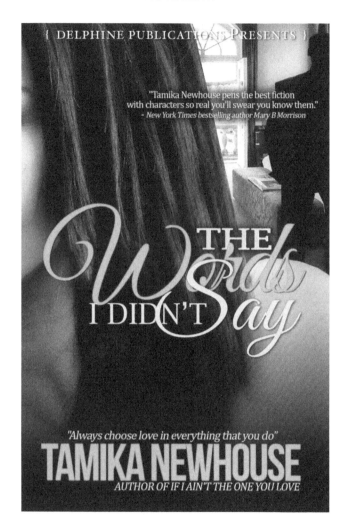

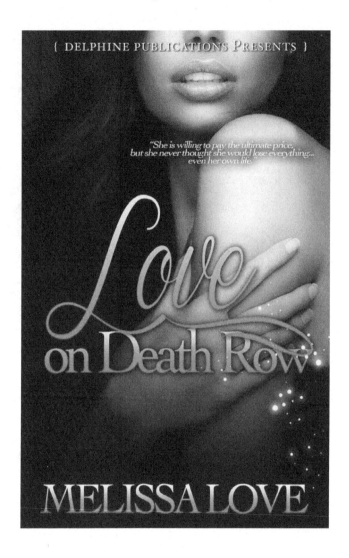

{ DELPHINE PUBLICATIONS PRESENTS }

"She is willing to pay the ultimate price,
but she never thought she would lose everything...
even her own life."

Love
on Death Row

MELISSA LOVE

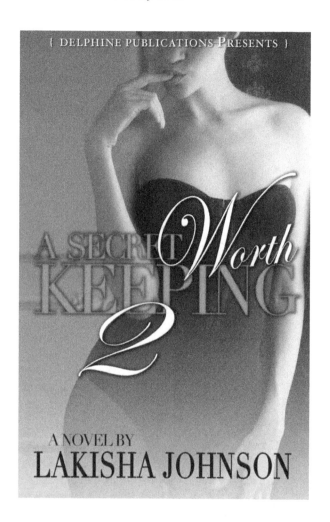

Made in the USA
Columbia, SC
18 July 2022

63643910R00143